Praise for

JUSTICE, INC.

"There is something immediately charming about Dale Bridges' prose. He is playful, but not unseriously so. He is experimental, but not in a way that ignores meaningful human interaction. I admire Bridges as a thinker — and he does think in his fiction, which is rare — and I do envy the range of his intelligence and talent. This first book is a shot across the bow of our culture. He will write many more, but read this one first."

Okla Elliott, author of *The Cartographer's Ink* and *From the Crooked Timber*

"*Justice, Inc.* may seem to be about robots, zombies, and clones, but it's actually about you and me. In the grand tradition of Tom Robbins and Christopher Moore, Bridges' wonderful collection of short stories brings to life fantastical worlds that allow us to laugh and cry about our own."

Joel Warner, co-author of *The Humor Code: A Global Search for What Makes Things Funny*

"Dale Bridges writes not with a pen but a skewer, piercing the absurdity of our cosmic sitcom with clarity and humor. *Justice, Inc.* is philosophical satire in the vein of Kurt Vonnegut and George Saunders — fellow madmen who have stared into the abyss and come away laughing. Be warned that there is a fifth

steed of the apocalypse, and its name is Justice — and Bridges
is lashing the whip, breathing fire, and coming for us all."

**Vince Darcangelo, editor of *Transgress* magazine and
the literary blog *Ensuing Chapters***

"*Justice, Inc.* is a book I wish I had written, a book George
Saunders could have written and a book Dale Bridges did
write. The characters in these stories are people pushed to the
limits of their existence by a future we never expected, a world
where technology and capitalism have pushed them against
the wall. Bridges captures that conflict perfectly. I hope I'm
dead and gone before Bridges' world becomes truth — it's
already happening."

**Jason Hardung, author of *The Broken and the Damned*
and *The Names of Lost Things***

"Dale writes with humor and wit about society's grim future.
He examines our moral compass with a keen eye, throwing
zombies, clones, and robotics at an apathetic world that has
lost its way."

The Masters Review

"I read the entire collection in one feverish sitting, marveling
as shit just kept getting weirder and weirder, and by the end, I
felt like I was reading a dystopian masterpiece."

Ariana D. Den Bleyker, Founder and Editor-in-Chief of

ELJ Publications, LLC and author of *Hatched from Bone, My Father Had a Daughter, Naked Animal,* and many more collections

"If artists are the antennae of the race, and Bridges is the voice of reason, it's clear we're all damned. In the age of slick formula fiction, the author breathes refreshing new life into the short story form. These are bizarre times, and Bridges attacks them with a brutal sense of humor and a savage pen. Here's an original writer who's going places."

Ben Corbett, author of *This is Cuba: An Outlaw Culture Survives*

"Welcome to the future. Ubiquitous . . . Ruminative . . . Baleful. Three words that people almost never say in real life, but whose meanings apply rather nicely to this book. In *Justice, Inc.* Dale Bridges looks into present day society vs. the fate of humanity and deals out a mighty helping of 'What If' stories, plunging pen first into futuristic pools to explore the big ticket items like mortality, where babies come from, and the endless complications involved with having a girlfriend. Sturgeon's Law states that 90% of pretty much everything is friable crap (Long Live Statistics!). Triumphantly, *Justice, Inc.* lives on the flipside in that remaining 10%."

Rob Geisen, author of *The Aftermath, etc.*

"The setting of *Justice, Inc.* is a terrifying near future where babies come in boxes, girlfriends are assembled, giant retailers adopt orphans and people live forever. Bridges examines the full consequences of these alternate futures with vivid characters, sparkling dialogue, and beautifully constructed plots. Bridges brings both a gallows humor and a sense of desperation to these tales that only heightens our awareness that the intersection of our fears and our technology just might bring us into this world."

Arsen Kashkashian, *Kash's Book Corner*

"Funny, vivid, brutal — who knew the next godpiss George Saunders was living in Texas and working at a used bookstore? p.s. I hope the future doesn't look remotely like this."

Steve Knopper, author of *Appetite for Self-Destruction: The Spectacular Crash of the Record Industry in the Digital Age* and freelance writer for the *New York Times, Rolling Stone,* and *Wired*

"The mark of a real short story artist is the ability to pull high impact with the fewest number of words, so every word must count no matter what the length — and Dale Bridges more than proves his prowess in this field. If it's out-of-the-box thinking you're looking for and a wry, gritty observational tone that skirts the edges of social offense and humor, *Justice, Inc.* is just the ticket. Expect the unexpected, for it's the norm in each story of Dale Bridges's hard-hitting collection."

Midwest Book Review

"Dale Bridges attacks the hollow pillars of consumerism and materialism and does so with the sharp know-how of a wizened satirist. This book will keep you laughing as much as it will question the direction of the society you inhabit."

David Accomazzo, *Phoenix New Times*

"Dale Bridges' story collection is a surreal blast of ridiculous mortals in post-apocalyptic situations, reminiscent of Saunders. It is rich and humorous, capturing unmitigated humanity at its most absurd. Strange, magnetic, and irresistible!"

Meg Tuite, author of *Bound by Blue* and fiction editor at *Connotation Press*

"If you've read and understood works by Etgar Keret, Julio Cortazar or Philip K. Dick you're bound to fall in love with Dale Bridges' *Justice, Inc.*"

Anthony ILacqua, author of *Undertakers of Rain* and editor-in-chief of *Umbrella Factory Magazine*

"If this is the future of dystopian fiction, the future is looking damn good!"

Kelly Smith, *Kelly Smith Reviews*

JUSTICE, INC.

DALE BRIDGES

MONKEY PUZZLE PRESS
HARRISON, ARKANSAS

COVER ART & DESIGN

Jay Miller

INTERIOR DESIGN

Nate Jordon

ISBN-10: 0-9915429-5-9
ISBN-13: 978-0-9915429-5-6

MONKEY PUZZLE PRESS
807 S. Oak St. Ste. 3
Harrison, AR 72601
monkeypuzzlepress.com

For Chris and Megan, my first readers.

TABLE OF CONTENTS

IN THE BEGINNING: AN INTRODUCTION

Imagine this. God creates a world. He makes it blue and green and round like a shiny marble. Then He takes a nap. When He wakes up, there are a bunch of fleshy bipeds running all over the place, naming things and bossing everyone around. God tells them to keep it down. They refuse. So He floods the marble. A few of the fleshy bipeds build a boat and make it out alive. God decides they can't do much harm and goes back to bed. Once again, He is awakened by their whining. He doesn't know how they got His number, but they are calling Him day and night. They don't want to build pyramids any longer. They want to live in a lactating country filled with bees. He sends them to Utah hoping to shut them up. God takes a Valium and crawls back into His pajamas. He tells His son to take all His calls. When He comes to, there are more fleshy bipeds than ever, and His son is nailed to a wooden "t." It isn't even a capital "T." God decides He needs a vacation. He puts the universe on autopilot and hops the next plane to Acapulco. He comes home, refreshed and tanned, only to find one group of fleshy bipeds dropping a fat, metal can of death on another group of fleshy bipeds. This gives God an idea. He decides there will be no peace until the fleshy bipeds are gone. Reasoning with them was pointless, His attempts to drown them had failed, and giving them what they wanted only seemed to make things worse. On the other hand, when left to their own devices, they appeared to do a fair job of exterminating themselves. So God kicks off his shoes, plops down on the sofa with a beer, and begins watching the divine sitcom He has inadvertently created.

In the year of our Lord 2014, a drunken, unemployed writer named Dale Bridges was attempting to steal cable from his neighbor in order to watch late-night porn and accidentally tapped into God's satellite feed. At first, Dale was upset there were no naked ladies on his television screen, but eventually he calmed down and took notice. A plagiarist by nature, he immediately began writing down the prophecies he saw. Several months later, he sent his writing off to a publisher and out came a book. He called it *Justice, Inc.*

This is that book, in case you're wondering. If you don't like it, take it up with God.

WELCOME TO OMNI-MART

Barry wants me to terminate the babies in the morning before the customers arrive, and he's the District Manager, so that's what I do. I wake up at 5 AM and I go to the Family Education Department and I remove all the InstaBabies from the shelves. I open each package from the top, as per the instructions on the back of the box, and I pull the cords marked "Bring Me to Life." In less than five minutes there are two dozen fat, multi-racial babies crying on the floor in front of me. They are very loud and I am afraid someone will report the disturbance to the national office and I will receive a negative comment on my bi-quarterly performance evaluation. I run around in a panic, making silly faces and cooing noises to distract them, but it doesn't do any good. Finally, I give up. Inside every box there is a small, silver key and on the back of every baby's head there is a keyhole. To terminate an InstaBaby, all you have to do is put the key in the hole and turn it to the right. The product immediately disintegrates into a fine white powder that can be swept up and thrown away. It's a simple procedure.

The InstaBaby was created by the Nuclear Family Corporation, which specializes in merchandise that "encourages good, old-fashioned American values." The target market for the InstaBaby is white mothers in their early forties who have a pathological fear that their teenage daughters will become impregnated out of wedlock by black men. This is a surprisingly large market. InstaBabies are designed to show these teenage daughters how difficult it is for a single mother to raise a multi-racial child in our society. After their Bring-Me-to-Life cords have been pulled, InstaBabies grow from infants to adults in the span of a single day. They bond with their caregivers and will not leave their side during that period. The teenage girl is forced to look after the InstaBaby during this time, and the experience is supposed to teach her valuable lessons about sexual promiscuity and social norms.

But there have been setbacks.

Apparently, instead of discovering that raising a multi-racial child is difficult, some teenage girls don't mind it all that much. Others even enjoy the experience. In Connecticut, a customer reported that her daughter never even considered dating an African-American male until she spent time with an InstaBaby. Now she is going steady with a black classmate and the mother has filed a 261-P Customer Grievance Report.

There have also been accounts of sexual deviants purchasing InstaBabies and using them for God-knows-what. Ex-convicts were taking out loans and buying them by the hundreds. Snuff films were circulated on the Internet. Dungeons were uncovered by local news stations. Charges were filed, but the courts were powerless to do anything to stop it. After all, InstaBabies aren't human. They are commercial items, pieces of property, like bicycles or frying pans. New regulations were created, but the PR damage had already been done.

Of course, the Nuclear Family Corporation quickly

recalled the defective product, which is why I am standing here at this unreasonable hour, trying to figure out which key goes to which head.

Destroying babies is not exactly in my job description, but Barry likes to assign me demeaning tasks. He enjoys reminding me that I belong to Omni-Mart, Inc. and am therefore legally obligated to follow his orders. I have known Barry since he was a pimple-faced bagboy, a sad wisp of hair on his upper lip, so skinny he could barely push an empty shopping cart down the aisle. I once caught him smoking pot and looking at dirty magazines in the Adult Fantasy Department, and he literally pissed himself when I said I was going to file a 560-G Employee Incident Report. But in the end, I couldn't do it. He looked so pathetic standing there in his urine-stained khakis—I didn't have the heart. Instead, I gave him a lecture on proper work-place conduct. I quoted from the *Omni-Mart Code of Employee Ethics* and reminded him that he was an Omni-Man and should behave accordingly. I don't think he liked being reprimanded that way by a lowly Lifetime Service Associate, but I had him by the short hairs and he knew it.

That was eight years ago. Perhaps I went a little overboard with my admonishments. Soon after, Barry started taking weight gainer and attending night classes in the managerial program. He purchased a body-building kit from the Male Fitness Department. His muscles began to stretch the cotton fibers of his official company smock, and he memorized every paragraph in the *Omni-Mart Manual of Conduct and Procedures*. If I'd known then he was going to grow up to be the size of a truck and become District Manager, I probably would have filed the 560-G and had his scrawny sixteen-year-old butt fired on the spot. But foresight has never been my strong suit.

Barry has never mentioned the peeing-in-his-pants incident, but I know he resents me for it and enjoys making me grovel. I have learned to live with the humiliation because, quite honestly, what other choice do I have? It's either this or The Outside, and no one wants to be on The Outside these days. So I deal with it the best way I know how. Barry says clean the toilets and I clean the toilets. Barry says destroy the babies and I destroy the babies.

By the time Omni-Mart officially opens, I have terminated all the InstaBabies except one, a quiet moon-faced child who is now approximately three years old. The label on the box says his name is Peter. When I approach Peter with the key, he does not run or cry. Instead, he reaches for me with pudgy hands and says, "Daddy."

Now, I am not a sentimental fool. I know this is not a real human child. This is just an extremely sophisticated toy that will turn to dust in less than eighteen hours. On the other hand, I am a very lonely man. I am forty-two years old and I do not have a family. My parents were poor, and, as is often the case in these types of situations, I was officially adopted by Omni-Mart, Inc. shortly after I was born. I have spent my entire life inside these walls. I am not complaining. These are tough times and I am lucky to have this kind of job security. I sleep in the Linens & Beddings Department and I have a substantial 401(k) plan. I sweep, I dust, I stock shelves. But sometimes I feel there should be more to life than this. I do not know what "more" would involve. After all, I have food, shelter, and satellite television. Omni-Mart carries every man-made product on the planet. I want for nothing. And yet, there is a yearning deep down in my chest late at night, like a fist squeezing my heart, and sometimes I wake up in a cold sweat.

I don't know what all of this has to do with a lifelike facsimile of a young, multi-racial boy, but I cannot bring myself to turn the final key. I decide I am going to stand up to Barry, which is something I have not done since he became District Manager. I will look him straight in his bulging, bloodshot eyes and tell him I have disobeyed his orders. I will say that he can go ahead and write a negative comment in my bi-quarterly performance evaluation and send it to the national office if he wants to, but I will not budge. Omni-Mart may be my legal guardian but they do not own my soul. I am a human being.

But when Barry finally arrives, I chicken out and hide Peter inside a rubber trashcan and tell him to keep quiet if he knows what's good for him.

"Welcome to Omni-Mart," says Barry.

"Welcome to Omni-Mart," I say.

He leans in close. I can smell his musky cologne and the protein shake he drank for breakfast. "Did you take care of that little problem?" he asks.

"Of course," I say.

When Barry nods his Rottweiler head, the ropey muscles in his neck contract like metal cables on a suspension bridge. "Very good. So the problem is taken care of?"

"Taken care of."

"*Completely* taken care of?"

"Completely."

He stabs me in the chest with a meaty finger. "For your sake I hope so, big guy. Don't forget that you're an official member of the Omni-Mart family, and you know what happens to family members who don't follow procedure. You don't want to end up like Terrance Omni."

Terrance Omni was a Lifetime Service Associate who worked in the Wicker Furniture Department, and two weeks before his retirement Barry caught him taking an unauthorized cigarette break in the Sanitation Room. Following an emergency performance evaluation, Terrance was stripped of his nametag and ejected into the back parking lot, where he lived inside a cardboard box for three weeks before he was anally violated and then kidnapped by a roving gang of teenage psychotics. We watched it all happen on the security cameras. No one has heard from Terrance since.

I give Barry my very best customer-service smile and tell him he has nothing to worry about, all the InstaBabies have been terminated. He glares at me and says I had better be telling him the truth. He says he's going to keep an eye on me. He says there's a clearance special in the Elderly Hygiene Department and I should get my ass down there pronto to demonstrate how to use our new line of adult diapers.

After Barry leaves, I lift Peter out of the trashcan and give him a lecture on how to treat his fellow man. I tell him all humans are created equal and should be handled with dignity and respect. Just because you're a large, muscular supervisor doesn't give you the right to be an asshole. I tell Peter that when dealing with someone like Barry, humility is important. And patience. And kindness. And if that doesn't work, you can always spit in their coffee.

Peter nods and says, "Always spit in their coffee."

As part of the parental simulation experience, InstaBabies are designed to mimic the behaviors and speech patterns of their caregiver. Eventually, Peter will adopt as much of my exterior personality as the hard drive in his little head can hold. I am not accustomed to anyone paying attention to what I say, and even though I know it's just a recording device triggered by a computer chip, hearing Peter repeat my words is sort of shocking to me. All day long, I take orders from customers and employers. I am told what to say and how to act. No one ever listens to my problems. No one actually cares how I feel about my job, my life. *Do you have vegan dog food?* That's what people want to know. *Does this remote-control espresso machine come with a warranty? Can I use this steak knife to cut burlap?* These are the type of questions I get. *Where is the Romantic Gestures Department?*

The Romantic Gestures Department is on the forty-fourth floor, section H-197B. It is where Cynthia Omni works, who is the woman I have been in love with since she was transferred here from Orlando five years ago. I spend all of my personal activity minutes in the Romantic Gestures Department. Like me, Cynthia is a Lifetime Service Associate, but unlike me, she once lived on The Outside. Her parents were successful orchid growers in Florida until the synthetic flower industry put them out of business and they were forced to sell their children to corporate buyers to prevent the family from starving to death. Cynthia's parents then starved to death. She's still bitter about it. She speaks often of her childhood on the farm, the fresh air, the sunshine. It sounds terrifying to me, but Cynthia assures me it was all quite pleasant.

"Welcome to Omni-Mart," I say.

"Welcome to Omni-Mart," says Peter.

"Yeah, yeah, yeah," says Cynthia.

Cynthia is wearing the emerald-green vest designating her as a female LSA. Her chaotic red hair has been tamed into a tight bun in accordance with the *Omni-Mart Dress Code Manual*, but her blue eyes still snap with cold fire. She looks at Peter, who is standing beside me holding on to my shirt sleeve. "And who is this?" she says.

"No one," I say. "Just a lost little boy looking for his parents." I look at Peter and nod my head vigorously. "Isn't that right?"

He doesn't miss a beat. "Just a lost little boy looking for his parents," Peter says.

Cynthia laughs, causing my heart to flip-flop in my chest. I have never told Cynthia I love her. Romantic relationships between employees are forbidden according to Section 85:6 of the *Omni-Mart Code of Employee Ethics*. Section 85:7 forbids romantic relationships between employees and customers. This is not such a burden for most workers, but it is practically unbearable for Lifetime Service Associates, who are not allowed to leave the facility. It means that, essentially, all romantic relationships are forbidden. If Barry ever gets proof that I have an unauthorized emotional attachment to Cynthia, you can bet I'll be out of a job faster than you can say "Please don't violate my anus."

Instead of telling Cynthia I love her, I buy orchids. Lots and lots of orchids.

Cynthia's job is to arrange synthetic flowers. She makes the most beautiful bouquets. Her tiny hands move amongst the blooms like hummingbirds searching for nectar. The walls of her work station are decorated with giant murals depicting idyllic mountain scenes complete with babbling brooks and majestic evergreens and happy chipmunks foraging for acorns, etc., etc. Whenever I visit, I can't look at the murals. I have to keep my attention focused very hard on Cynthia or I will start to hyperventilate and pass out. Dr. Peterson in the Pharmaceutical Solutions Department says I have the worst case of agoraphobia he has ever seen. He says even the thought of The Outside is enough to put me in a psychological coma. I can't handle open spaces. Green meadows cause me to break out in hives. Blue skies make me nauseous. To alleviate this problem, Doc prescribes various drugs and frequent sessions in his Isolation Chamber, which is a small, black box with a breathing tube that shuts out all light and sound. As Dr. Peterson says, "The world can't hurt you if it can't find you." The only time I feel completely safe outside of the Isolation Chamber is when I'm watching Cynthia arrange flowers, but even then I have to be careful not to look at the murals.

To say Cynthia hates the synthetic flower industry would be a gross understatement. She blames them for the death of her parents. But Omni-Mart does not acknowledge personal preferences when considering employee assignments. They simply look at your skills chart and match you with the most appropriate department. Cynthia got the Romantic Gestures Department. I got the Miscellaneous Assignments Department.

As we walk down the aisle, Cynthia identifies certain species of synthetic orchids and recites the prescribed customer information data for each one. I pick one of every species she identifies. Peter—now almost twelve years old—walks next to me, smiling and repeating every word Cynthia says. Soon Cynthia becomes annoyed with this and tells Peter to shut up.

Which he does. However, this also seems to annoy her. "What's wrong with that kid?" she whispers to me.

I shrug. "What do you mean?"

"I don't know. He just seems far too obedient for a boy his age."

I tell her that he is just polite and accommodating. What's wrong with doing what you're told? What's wrong with being a compliant young boy?

Cynthia shakes her head. "OK, OK. Don't get your panties in a bunch, Mr. Omni. I just think the kid is kind of creepy, that's all."

At the end of our walk, I have an armful of synthetic orchids, which Cynthia makes into a bouquet. I pay for the flowers with my monthly credit allowance. Cynthia informs her supervisor that she is going to take fifteen personal activity minutes, and we all go down to the Sanitation Room. The Sanitation Room is pretty much what it sounds like: a room where trash is disposed of in giant incinerators. I place the flowers inside one of the dormant incinerators and shut the door. I show Peter how to press the POWER button, and we all watch through the viewing window as the orange-blue flames ignite, turning the fake orchids into a heap of black ash in just a few short seconds. Cynthia smiles and my heart flipflops once again. We do this at least once a month, but I'd do it every day if I could afford it.

Without saying a word, Cynthia reaches over and slips her hand into mine. Her skin is dry and cool and flawless. I am ecstatic. And yet, I can't help glancing repeatedly at the door. This is a clear violation of company policy. If one of Barry's cronies were to walk in right now, I would definitely be terminated on the spot. Cynthia doesn't believe it, but Barry has a crush on her. Every time Cynthia walks into the room, Barry finds an excuse to flex his muscles. Sometimes he lifts heavy objects for no particular reason and then sets them back on the ground, like a bored gorilla in the zoo. It's kind of funny but also kind of scary, because I am afraid someday Cynthia will look at Barry's giant muscles and then look at my scrawny muscles and say to herself, What have I been thinking?

I hold on to Cynthia's hand for as long as I can stand it, and then I let go, sick to my stomach at my own cowardice.

Cynthia sighs and leans in close, her breath tickling the graying hairs in my ear. "I want to leave," she says for the millionth time. "I can't stand it here."

I can't look at her, so I stare at the orchid ashes in the incinerator instead.

"It's just not a good time right now," I say.

"It's never a good time. That's the point. You just have to take a chance, cowboy."

"We'll go soon, I promise. I just need to get organized. I want to be prepared."

Cynthia sighs. She steps in front of me, grabs the back of my head, and forces my mouth onto hers. She is much stronger than she looks. Our teeth sound like tiny tap shoes when they click together. I can smell the apple-scented shampoo from the Hair Supplies Department and taste the cherry-flavored lipstick from the Facial Cosmetics Department. "I love you, Leonard," she says fiercely.

My heart pounds in my chest and I want to take her in my arms and return her kiss and tell her I love her over and over again. Instead, I give her all the usual excuses why it's a bad time to leave. I tell her we have no money. I tell her it's the rainy season. I remind her of all the dangers on The

Outside that have been reported in the news. War. Poverty. Famine. Violence. Besides, our life here isn't so bad. Why risk everything on an uncertain future? We should be thankful for what we have, right?

When I finish my little spiel, Cynthia kisses me on the cheek and says, "You are a good man, Leonard. But you are weak. I can't wait forever, you know." She looks at Peter, who is obsessively pressing the POWER button on the incinerator. "And I don't know who this strange boy really is, but you'd better take him to the Lost & Found Department before Barry figures out what you're up to."

"I'm not afraid of Barry," I say.

"I'm not afraid of Barry," says Peter.

Cynthia rolls her eyes and then leaves without saying goodbye. I take a white handkerchief from my pocket and carefully wipe her lipstick from my cheek. I fold the handkerchief into a perfect square, and place it in the incinerator. Peter pushes the POWER button. The flames leap high.

Sometimes I see a nice elderly couple shopping in the facility and I imagine they are my parents returning to claim me. I imagine them holding me in their arms. I imagine tears of joy. I imagine Barry's reaction when they tell him I was stolen as a baby and sold to Omni-Mart illegally. I imagine Barry's large, red face turning even redder and his stuttering apology.

I wonder what they were like, my parents. Were they loveable, incompetent hippies with long hair and glassy eyes? Were they girthy, sincere small-town conservatives? Did they love me? Did my mother cry when they made the final decision? Did my father hold her and tell her it was all for the best?

My personnel file says I was discovered in the Office Supplies Department chewing on a stapler. I was wearing a diaper with a note attached to it. The note said, "His name is Leonard. We're so sorry."

Every year, hundreds of babies are lost or abandoned in Omni-Mart. Of course, every effort is made to locate the parents, but after six months, the courts allow the corporation to adopt the children instead of turning them over to a Family Replacement Facility. I was raised in the Lost & Found Department until the age of fifteen, and then I became a Lifetime Service Associate.

I could always resign of course. Cynthia keeps suggesting we run away together. It's a simple procedure—all we have to do is walk out the front door. But how do you quit the only family you've ever known? How do you quit your life?

All morning, Barry thinks of embarrassing tasks for me to perform and then he assigns them via the intercom so everyone can hear.

"Leonard Omni, please report to the Large Pets Department for a fecal-matter clean-up project. Thank you."

"Leonard Omni, please report to the Plus-Size Women's Department for a price check on a plus-size brassiere. Thank you."

The other employees used to snicker behind my back about the way Barry treats me. Now they do it right to my face. I have absolutely zero credibility as an authority figure.

This is what the memo from the national office said when I applied for the managerial program last month. The word "ZERO" was in all caps, which I thought was unnecessary. I wrote a long, impassioned response memo stating that leadership is not just about authority. There's also empathy and communication and developing a genuine connection to the people you're working with. Isn't there more to life than productivity? What about respect for the individual? What about basic human decency?

In response, the national office sent me a fifteen-dollar gift certificate and told me to apply again next year.

At noon, Cynthia and I meet in the Frozen Foods Department, as usual, and select our meals from the endless aisles of rectangular freezers. Peter is now in his mid-thirties and slightly taller than I am. His skin is the color of milky coffee and he has a beautiful head of springy, black hair. I have given him a company uniform to wear and he is happy following me around the store learning every detail about my life. Obviously, Cynthia knows there's something odd about the situation, but she has decided stay out of it. The hard drive in Peter's head has absorbed my words, my facial features, my gestures, and he now predicts what I am going to say and do with disturbing accuracy. At times, I think Peter's impersonation of me is better than the real thing.

While we eat, news reports about The Outside flash across the video-dome above our heads, each one sponsored by an advertiser. TEXAS AND CALIFORNIA AT WAR AGAIN. *Enjoy Coke!* WEAPONS OF MASS DESTRUCTION

FOUND IN BROOKLYN. *You're in good hands with All-State.* TIGER ESCAPES FROM ZOO, MAULS CHILD. *Beef, it's what's for dinner.*

I am halfway through my frozen chicken-fried chicken substitute when Barry shows up with his usual smirk.

"Welcome to Omni-Mart," says Barry.

"Welcome to Omni-Mart," I say.

"Welcome to Omni-Mart," says Peter.

Cynthia stuffs a forkful of ravioli in her mouth.

"So, Cynthia, still hanging out with the non-managerial losers, eh?" Barry says. He laughs too loudly and slaps me on the back, practically crushing my vertebrae. "Just kidding, big guy. You know I like to pal around with my employees."

"Ha ha," I say. "That's a good one, Barry."

Barry nods and leans against a display rack in a way that makes his triceps bulge.

"Technically, we're not your employees," says Cynthia, ignoring Barry's bulgy triceps. "We are employed by the Omni-Mart Corporation."

Barry forces a smile and leans harder against the display rack. "Of course, of course. But I am the *Manager.*"

"*District* Manager," says Cynthia. "Omni-Mart is a global operation, and there are literally thousands of managerial positions." Barry's face reddens as Cynthia begins to list all the supervisors who have authority over him in the facility. "There's the Area Manager and the Section Manager and the Regional Manager and the Locality Manager and the Province Manager and the Operations Manager and the Utilities Manager and the Custodial Manager—"

"And the Lifetime Service Associates," Barry interrupts. He folds his arms across his massive chest and begins to bounce his pectorals up and down one after the other. Right, left, right, left, right, left. . . . It looks like there are two nippled pistons firing away under his shirt. "You know, some people say the Lifers are expendable, but not me. No, siree-bob. We couldn't function without someone to perform the menial labor. It's the common people—like you two—that keep this company running."

"I am also a Lifetime Service Associate," says Peter.

Barry turns his attention to Peter for the first time. My heart drumrolls in my chest.

"So you are," says Barry. "And how's that working out for you?"

"Very well," says Peter. "It is an honor to be a member of the Omni-Mart family. Omni-Mart is more than a corporation; it is a community. We hope to make the world a better place one customer at a time."

Cynthia sticks her index finger down her throat and pretends to gag. I pray Barry doesn't move to the other side of the table and see the keyhole on the back of Peter's head.

"I like your attitude," says Barry. "What'd you say your name was?"

"Peter Omni."

"Right. You've got gumption, Peter. How long have you been working for us?"

"My whole life."

"Well, don't give up. If you work hard, maybe you'll follow in my footsteps one day."

"That's my goal," says Peter.

"That's bullshit."

The words are out of my mouth before I can stop them. I freeze, horrified. Cynthia smiles.

"Excuse me, Leonard," says Barry. "Was anyone talking to you?"

"No, they were not," I say. "I'm very sorry. I apologize. I'm sorry."

"Do you have a problem with Peter wanting to follow in my footsteps?"

"No. It's a worthy ambition. I'm sorry."

"Is there something funny about an employee who wants to make something out of his career instead of pissing it away sweeping floors and stocking shelves?"

"Not at all. I'm sorry."

"Then why did you interrupt our conversation?"

Barry stares at me. Peter stares at me. Cynthia stares at me. What can I say? I can't tell them the truth. I can't say that Peter is a high-tech product designed to emulate me in every way. I can't say that Peter is probably the closest thing I will ever have to a son. I can't tell them Peter's desire to become Barry insinuates my own desire to become Barry, a thought so repugnant it made me blurt out two inappropriate words. I can't tell them I fear Omni-Mart does not just own the rights to my life, they own the rights to my character as well. I can't tell them that every night I pray to a God I don't believe in that I will suddenly find the courage to burn this whole place to the ground and salt the earth it sits upon. I can't tell them that. Can I? No, I cannot. And I do not.

"I'm so very sorry," I say instead.

Barry smiles in a way that makes my stomach drop.

"That's OK, big guy," he says. He clamps a giant paw on my shoulder and squeezes until I'm sure I feel a few ligaments pop. "Hey, I just remembered. I have another job for you. How do you feel about windows?"

The older kids in the Lost & Found Department used to tell stories about The Outside. One of them was about a wolf that ate little girls dressed in red hoods. Another was about a witch who lived in a house made of gingerbread. I didn't believe the stories, of course, but they frightened me anyhow. The Outside was so big, so unknowable, that every type of imaginable horror seemed possible.

One night, the bigger kids came to my bed while I was sleeping and kidnapped me. They tied me up and threw me into the parking lot behind the facility. I was trapped on The Outside for almost eight hours before one of the Pre-Employee Caretakers discovered I was missing. This happens all the time. Call it an initiation if you want. Call it hazing, call it torture, call it boys will be boys. Whatever. It happens.

It was the middle of August, and there was a lightning storm. The sky was pitch black and every couple of seconds a giant bolt of electricity would snake out of the clouds, followed by a loud roar. I had never experienced lightning or thunder or a pitch-black sky, and I guess I had a small breakdown. I'm not exactly sure what happened next. When I woke up, I was tied to a bed screaming at the top of my lungs. The other kids said customers could hear me all the way over in the Ethnic Shoes Department, although that seems unlikely. The Caretakers tried to make me explain what happened, but I told them I couldn't remember. I said I blacked out.

But that's a lie. I remember.

There was something out there in the darkness. I can't say what it was exactly, but it was there. A wolf? A witch? It had wings and teeth and claws shaped like sharpened question marks. It came up behind me and sniffed my hair. It licked my neck with a long, pink tongue. I shut my eyes tight and started to cry. At first, I thought it was all just my imagination. Then I realized it was *definitely* my imagination. That's when I went berserk. If The Outside was actually inside my head, it was even more dangerous than I thought. It was everywhere and it was nowhere. It was infinite.

I knew right then I would never leave Omni-Mart. I screamed and screamed.

Barry takes me to the Observation Room, which is a room at the very top of the facility where customers go to look at The Outside. Every wall is made of double-plated glass. I have heard about the Observation Room but I have never been there. Even the thought of it turns my legs to noodles. As soon as we step off the elevator, I catch a glimpse of the sunlight gleaming through the giant windows, and I close my eyes tight. I fall to my knees. Vomit rises in my throat.

Barry puts a wet rag in my hand and says "Clean." I try to talk him out of it. I tell him I'm not feeling well. He says "Clean." I tell him I have a bad back. He says "Clean." I tell him I am frightened, I am lonely, I am desperate, oh God, I'm scared to death. He says "Clean."

I take the rag and crawl forward with my eyes still shut. I reach a slick, smooth surface and I start to wipe it with the rag. I am shaking uncontrollably.

"You can't clean like that," says Barry. "Open your eyes, big guy. You have to open your eyes."

I do. I open my eyes and look at The Outside. I am surrounded by an endless city filled with terror at every turn. I see metal vehicles hurtling through the streets and imminent death on every corner. I see a dirty, unconscious man on the ground below. I see another man kick the unconscious man and take his wallet. I see a woman begging for money. Next to the woman there is a baby in a stroller. I see poverty. I see violence. I see death. Off in the distance, I do see the outlines of mountains, but they are hopelessly far away. I don't see trees or rivers or playful chipmunks. There is only the city, with its labyrinthine buildings and factories, and beyond, more city, more buildings and factories, more Omni-Marts. This is the result of human progress. This is what people working together towards a common goal can accomplish. I feel a warm chill in the crotch of my pants and I look down to see a puddle of urine accumulating on the floor beneath me.

"Oh, my. What is this?" says Barry. "It looks like Leonard Omni has pissed his pants. I don't think that's how an Omni-Man should behave, Leonard, do you? Clean it up."

Barry puts his hand on the back of my neck and shoves my face toward the puddle, as if I am an incontinent dog that has had an accident in the house. I choke back a sob and start to mop up my bodily fluids, but I don't get far. Spots dance before my eyes and I begin to hyperventilate. The room shrinks. My vision blurs. I pass out.

When I wake up, I'm in a hospital bed again, but at least I'm not screaming this time. Peter is standing next to me. I must have been out for a long time because Peter looks ancient. He is almost completely bald and his skin is brittle and wrinkled like tissue paper.

"Welcome to Omni-Mart," says Peter.

"Welcome to Omni-Mart," I say. "Where's Cynthia?"

"She is gone."

I sit up. There are dozens of plastic tubes sticking out of me. "Gone where?"

"She has been sent to The Outside. She has been terminated."

I start to pull out the tubes. "Terminated? For what?"

"Section eighty-five six of the *Omni Code of Employee Ethics*. Romantic relationships between employees are forbidden."

I am stunned. "But we didn't do anything. I followed procedure. How could they know?"

"She was disloyal," says Peter. "This is what you wanted. It is all for the best."

For the first time, I look deep into Peter's eyes and notice how shiny and lifeless they are. They are like two polished, alabaster marbles encased in wax. I stare into them intently and see my own disfigured, convex reflection looking back at me. In that moment, something small yet important snaps inside me.

"What have you done?" I say.

Peter cocks his head. "I did what you would have done if you were me."

I grab Peter by the throat and tell him to explain. He looks vaguely surprised, and he talks quickly. Peter says that after I passed out, he told the national office what happened in the Sanitation Room. How Cynthia kissed me and I ignored her. How Cynthia said she loved me and I soundly rejected her. How I remained loyal to Omni-Mart at all costs. How I followed procedure. He tells me Barry called Cynthia in for an emergency performance evaluation and asked her if she loved me. Cynthia said "Yes." Barry called in the Regulations Manager from the national office and asked Cynthia again if she loved me. Cynthia said "Yes." Barry fired her immediately with the Regulations Manager's approval. She was stripped of her nametag and ejected into the back parking lot.

When he finishes, I notice my fingers have broken through the plastic skin on Peter's neck. If he had been human, I would have murdered him. I take the silver key from my pocket and tell Peter I'm going to terminate him once and for all. "I regret your existence," I say, although this is not entirely true. "I regret your existence," Peter repeats. He turns around so I have access to the keyhole. My hand is shaking, but I manage to perform the deed anyhow. I insert the key and turn it to the right. The product immediately disintegrates into a fine, white powder that can be swept up and thrown away.

I put on my clothes and run to Barry's office. Of course, I am too late. Cynthia is gone. There is only Barry and the Regulations Manager. The Regulations Manager is a bald man wearing a suit that costs more than I make in a year. I know this because he says, "This suit costs more than you make in a year." He commends me on following procedure. Turning away Cynthia's advances demonstrates where my ultimate loyalties lie. He says he likes my gumption. He says I'm exactly the type of guy he wants to see in the managerial program. Barry protests, but the Regulations Manager cuts him off. "What do you say?" he asks me. "If you work hard, maybe you'll follow in my footsteps one day."

I should tell him to go to hell. I know I should. I should spit in his face and run out the front door screaming Cynthia's name. I should confront my fear of The Outside and find Cynthia and tell the world I love her.

Sadly, I do not. A lifetime of following orders has taken its toll. Instead, I accept the offer to enroll in the managerial program without much hesitation. I promise to become the best supervisor Omni-Mart, Inc. has ever seen. I even shake the Regulation Manager's hand and shed a tear. An honest-to-God tear. The look in Barry's eyes while all this is happening gives me more pleasure than I want to admit. No one should feel this much joy over a petty vindication, but I do. This is the greatest moment of my life.

I study hard and eventually become the Miscellaneous Assignments Manager at my franchise location. I am not an abusive supervisor like Barry. I treat my coworkers with dignity and patience, and I am well-loved by my staff. I earn the respect and admiration of my superiors in the national office, and I receive commendations for my efforts. I purchase numerous expensive suits that cost more than I used to make in a year. Since I am now a member of management, I am allowed to date whomever I want. Eventually, I marry a pretty, young clerk from the Paper Supplies Department and we have a child named Leslie. Leslie has her father's nose and her mother's delicate chin. I am allowed to leave the facility whenever I desire, but I choose to live in Omni-Mart. Management applauds my decision and walls off a substantial section of the Linens & Beddings Department. We have a splendid apartment stocked entirely with state-of-the-art Omni-Mart products. I work hard all day and come home to a loving family and a home-cooked meal. My wife and daughter think I'm a swell guy. Leslie adores her father and she wants to grow up and be just like me. Often, Leslie will follow me around repeating every word I say. Sometimes when my wife and daughter are sound asleep, I slip out of the apartment and take the elevator to the Observation Room. With the help of several new products from the Pharmaceutical Solutions Department, I have overcome my agoraphobia, and I can now look at the outside without much fear. At night, the city does not seem so hostile. All of the poverty, the filth, the violence is covered up by darkness and the trash fires resemble tiny Christmas lights blinking off and on. I stare at the streets below and wonder if one of those lights belongs to Cynthia. Is she waiting for me out there? Does she still have faith I will become the type of man she can respect?

I ride the elevator back down to my apartment. I kiss my beautiful daughter and slip into bed with my beautiful wife. There is no longer a yearning deep down in my chest late at night, like a fist squeezing my heart, and I do not wake up in cold sweats. I am not haunted by the desire to find my parents or risk my life for love. Those aspirations are gone and now there is nothing inside of me. Absolutely nothing. When I close my eyes, I feel the exact opposite of passion. I feel hopeless. I feel infinite. I feel like an Omni-Man.

TEXTING THE APOCALYPSE

hey ginger

hey brittany

u hear abowt the end of the werld?

yeah bummer

i know rite?

rite

fire and brimstone

yeah brimstone smelz like ick

totaly

btw ricky sutton talked 2 me 2day

no way

way

THE ricky sutton?

yeah

no way

way! way! way!

cool. just a sec. my parentz r totly freakin out abowt the zombies

yeah this apokalips is lame

tell me abowt it. yestrday my bro got fed to The Beast

the cute bro or the 1 w zits

cute

oh sorry

its k. i get his room

score!

i know

did u see the skirt jenny wore for the genocide?

i know. totaly 2012

yeah i was like, That skirt is totaly 2012!

good one

rite?

hey. gotta go. my stupid mom wants me to join a cult with her

which 1?

the 1 that eats fried twinkies and sacrifices newborn puppies
to tom cruise

cool. the tom-twinkie cult is the best. suzie is a membr

sweet. c u in hell

totaly

LIFE AFTER MEN

Danny's partially rotten head makes a totally grosso crunching noise when I smash it with my $2,000 Gucci handbag. He falls to the sidewalk and sort of flops around down there helplessly, while I stand over him, hands on hips, and glare. For a second, his spasms remind me of the last time we frogged, almost two months ago. *That* was not a pretty sight, either.

"Emily!" Tiffany screams at me. "What's your malfunction?"

She snatches the pink faux-leather purse away from me and tries to wipe the blood and brain matter off before it has a chance to dry. It doesn't work. She just ends up smearing everything around and making it about a gazillion times worse. She reaches inside the bag and pulls out the brick I've been carrying around all afternoon for this occasion.

"How many times have I told you to use the Ralph Lauren bag if you want to bash your boyfriend's skull in? That's why we have it, you little strump."

She tosses the purse into a nearby dumpster in disgust and then kicks Danny right in the goodies. Danny moans and rolls over on his stomach (also a move that reminds me of our sex life). Then, for no reason at all, Tiff goes totally nervy and starts to yell and kick him at the same time. *"That! Was! My! Favorite! Purse!"*

Tiffany has been a real blue-ribbon bitch lately. I wish I could say she's just having her mensies or something, but she doesn't cycle until next week. She's signed up to leave on one of the evacuation boats today, and she's all nervy because I won't go with her. As if. There's no way I'm getting on an oil tanker full of lezzies and sailing off to some godpiss island somewhere in the middle of the ocean. Nope. Not *this* necro bitch. I'd rather hide out here on the mainland and wait for a cure than hit the high seas with a bunch of nervy strumps.

Finally, Tiffany stops wailing on my ex long enough to take out her iPhone and check her messages. "What do you want to do now?" she asks, nodding towards Danny.

Obviously, the humane thing would be to put him out of his misery. I don't know if he feels any pain, but he's gushing blood like a stuck pig and making one hell of a mess. On the other hand, in order to dispose of him properly, we'd have to burn the body and then saw his head off and take it to a Bio Hazard Disposal Unit. By the time we finished filling out the godpiss paperwork, Tiffany would have to leave. And what kind of a send-off is that?

I shrug. "Wanna get a fruit smoothie?"

"You know it," Tiffany says. So we head off in the direction of Jamba Juice, leaving Danny to the whims of the Sanitation Commission.

I know he's not much to look at now, but Danny was a gorgeous hunk of man-meat when I first met him six months ago. For the reals. He had dimples all the way to China and these beautiful abs that bulged out all over his stomach like mini loaves of baked bread. Mmmmm. He was yummy. I wanted to frog his brains out the first time I saw him.

He picked me up at a bar called Stabs near the marina. Well, I let him *think* he picked me up. You know how beasties are—they want to make all the moves but they're too stupid to know when to frog and when to frog off. Danny wasn't the sharpest shank in the prison shower, so I practically had to sit on his godpiss face before he got the godpiss hint.

I had four months of mind-blowing, thank-you-Jesus, don't-tell-my-mom-I-do-that sex before he started to change. Tiffany warned me it would happen. She told me not to get too attached.

"It's great for a while," she said. "He'll bring you flowers every day and frog you like a water buffalo every night. He'll buy you those awful chocolate candies with the jizzy stuff in the middle. Then, after a couple of months, he'll start getting all nervy for no reason. When you want to talk about it, his eyes will glass over and he'll moan. Aaaaaaaaahhhh. The next thing you know, he's staying out with the boys all night long and coming home with blood stains on his collar. That's when you'll have to bash his head in, just like all the others."

"Shut up, whore," I said. "We can't all be frigid muff divers like you."

"Don't knock it until you try it," the strump replied.

Tiffany is always trying to get under my skin . . . and under my skirt. About a year ago, she joined this new cult—sorry, I mean "political interest group"—called Life After Men. As far as I can tell, the LAMs are just a bunch of New Age lezzies who sit around bitching about the patriarchal ideal of feminine beauty and stuffing their muzzles with high-carb, microwaveable snacks. Today, the LAMs are all getting on an evacuation boat together and sailing off to some all-vaj Xanadu somewhere in the Caribbean. No beasties allowed. Sounds about as fun as an ice-cold douche.

No one knows for sure why the virus only affects beasties, but the LAMs have a few theories on the subject. They think the virus triggers some sort of genetic mutation in the Y chromosome that shuts down the frontal lobe of the brain and turns all the good men into lobotomized monsters that act out their most basic instincts: frogging, killing, and eating, in that order. (Boys will be boys, as my mother used to say. Talk about a nervy strump.) According to the *LAM Manifesto*, the military was planning to use the virus to create an army of indestructible super soldiers, which is why women, homos, and pappies are immune.

Tiffany *says* she believes all this crap, but if you want to know the truth, I think she just goes along with it because she likes the attention. Tiffany is bi. At least, she used to be when we were growing up. These days, who knows? She hated beasties long before this virus thing came along and now I think she's trying to go straight vaj. Whatevs. I couldn't care less. There's no way I'm turning lezzie, though. Not on your life. Best friends or not, I like pole. One dick, two dicks. Black dicks, blue dicks. I love 'em all. Chop the foreskin off and I'll ride that rocket ship like Neil Frogging Armstrong, or keep it on and I'll snuggle down with a turtle neck. I'd rather be a necro lover than a camel-toe kisser any day.

I know she doesn't look like it, but Tiffany is kind of a freaky genius. Somehow, she just knows things, all kinds of things, pretty much everything there is to know, in fact.

I'm with her 24/7, and I never see her read anything more academic than *Cosmo*. It's like her brain was programmed at birth with all the information she would ever need.

For instance, there was this one time in seventh grade when she got into a big argument with our math teacher about the value of zero. Mr. Gustafson was one of those teachers all the boys liked and all the girls hated, primarily because he was a frogging perv. I always brought an extra sweatshirt to his class because no matter how many layers of clothing you had on that creepy beastie stared at you like you were naked. He really had it in for Tiffany, too. In fact, all our teachers hated Tiff. I'm not exactly sure why.

"Look," Mr. Gustafson told Tiffany once, as he held an apple in front of his bloated, scabby face. "This is *one* apple." He put his hands behind his back slowly, like he was attempting to explain a magic trick to a retarded kid. "Now, there are *zero* apples. It's very simple. Even a spoiled rich girl who spends all her time at the mall should be able to figure it out."

All the boys in the class went "OOOOOOHHH," just like the beasties always do when they smell public humiliation.

Tiffany smiled sweetly. "Actually, there's still *one* apple, dipshit," she said. "It's behind your back. Just because you can't see the apple doesn't, like, negate its existence. And even if you completely obliterate the apple, you don't have zero apples—you have nothing. Zero is not an actual number. It's a theoretical numeral we use for mathematical purposes. It's very simple. Even a second-rate junior high teacher who still lives with his mother should be able to figure that out."

See what I mean? We were twelve years old. Where the hell did she learn that? It's not like VH1 has a *Behind the Equations* special.

After Jamba Juice, Tiffany and I head down to the beach to snatch a few rays before her boat leaves. Infected beasties are sensitive to sunlight, so they never come out during the day. It has something to do with photosynthesis or melanin or something. Whatevs. I'm sure Tiffany knows. Since Danny was only a couple of months into the change, he was still about half human, which is why he could hang out with us. He bitched about it the whole time, though. "Oh, the sun hurts my eyes." "Oh, my skin is on fire." Finally, I just got sick of his nervy voice and decided to break up with him. Technically, the law says you're supposed to wait until they try to eat your brains before you take a whack at them, but what's the point? Once the magic is gone, get them before they get you—that's what I say.

The beach is filled with women, of course. Nervy lezzies, every one. There are a few homos playing in the water and a couple of pappies passed out like beached whales near the lifeguard chair, but besides that it's vaj as far as the eye can see. What a world.

"You want me to get your back?" Tiffany asks.

"Sure," I say, even though I know it's a trap. "But stay away from my fun hole, bitch. You're not on your lezzie island yet."

Tiffany rolls her eyes. "Whatever, strump. I'm not even attracted to you. You're too flat-chested. You look like a godpiss boy, for christsake"

I snort. "Don't try that reverse psychology crap on me. My girls may not be as big as yours, but they've got attitude. A-T-T-I-T-U-D, 'attitude.'"

"There's an E at the end of 'attitude,' you know."

"Yeah, and there's a TIT right in the middle. Now, make

with the sunscreen."

Tiffany squirts the cold white lotion onto my back, and you can almost hear all the lezzies wet themselves as they watch her rub it in. When she's done, we swap places and I do her. Afterwards, we get into tanning positions.

My eyes are closed for less than five godpiss minutes when the world suddenly goes dark. What the hell, I think, must be a frogging eclipse or something. Nope. It's just two LAMs hovering over us like vultures waiting for a snack. Standing next to one another, they cast a giant shadow in the shape of the number 10, the 0 blocking out all my sun.

They want Tiffany, of course. She's like their guru or messiah or something, and if they don't hear from her every twenty minutes, they freak out and form a search party. These two look like characters in a weird nursery-rhyme, the anorexic Jack Sprat and his enormous wife who can eat no lean. The head strump, Alice, has spiky pink hair, a nose ring, and fat rolls holding up her fat rolls. Her scrawny sidekick, Denise, has grosso blond dreadlocks, no chin, and the mournful eyes of a stray puppy starving in the rain. I've met them both before. Tiffany holds LAM meetings at the apartment all the time. Needless to say, they hate my frogging guts.

I push my sunglasses onto my forehead and smile up at them. "Hello, Alan. Hello, Dennis."

"My name is *Alice*," the bull moose says. She's wearing a two-piece bathing suit, although her gut hangs so low the second piece is MIA. "And this is *Denise*."

Denise picks up a seashell and pretends to examine it.

I push my shades back down. "Oh, right. Sorry."

Alice runs her nervy eyes over my thin, girlish figure and sneers. "It's not too late to sign up for the evacuation," she says. "Or are you still whoring around with the patriarchy?"

Tiffany puts up a warning hand, but it's too late.

"Thanks for the offer," I answer. "But I get seasick. You *can* do me a huge favor, though. You're, like, blocking all of my sun. Could you take a few steps back? Pretty please. Stomp your hoof once for yes and twice for no."

Alice grunts and makes a move like she's going to jump me. Which, considering she has the girth of a small planet, could be cause for alarm. Denise drops the seashell and starts digging in the sand with her toe.

"All right, girls. That's enough," Tiffany says. "What do you need, Alice?"

Alice stops glaring at me and answers Tiffany in a sugar-sweet voice. "All the supplies are loaded on the boat. We should get on board right now to make sure we get a seat."

"We have assigned seats," Tiffany answers. "And the ship doesn't leave for three hours. Why don't you take roll and double check the supply list? We can't just turn around and come back if we forget something, you know?"

Alice doesn't budge. It's obvious she'd rather use deodorant for the first time than leave Tiffany alone with me for even one moment. She looks at me with hate and suspicion. Now I know how Jonah felt right before the whale swallowed him.

"Oh, don't worry about me, *Alan*." I blow her a kiss. "I'll just wait right here until you get back, big boy."

Finally Alice spins on her heels and stomps away. Instead of weaving in and out of the people lying out on the beach, she marches in a straight line, scattering bikini-clad tourists everywhere like a nervy rhino charging through a herd of squirrels.

A soft, whimpering sound escapes from Denise's mouth.

At first I think she's crying, but then I see she's actually trying to talk.

"What are you saying?" I ask. Tiffany puts her hand on my shoulder but I shrug it off. "Speak up, you nervy strump. I can't hear you."

"You didn't need to be like that," says Denise quietly, looking down at her feet. "Alice isn't a bad person. She's only trying to understand you."

"And who asked her to do that?"

"No one."

"That's right. No one. You tell that fat cow to stay out of my business, you understand?"

Her eyes are big and blue and filled with salt water, like the ocean, and suddenly I see the whole story: Denise in love with Alice, mooning over her every day, while Alice moons over Tiffany and Tiffany moons over me and I moon over every frogging beastie on the planet that's trying to destroy me. It's not a love triangle; it's a love pentagram.

I have no idea why I get so nervy about the LAMS. It's not as though I've had such great experiences with men my whole life. My dad was a drunk, my brother was a rapey perv, and all my boyfriends were violent bastards even before the virus came along. But you know how it is—old habits blah blah blah. I love Tiffany more than she will ever know, but I can't tell her that. She needs to leave. I need her to go. It's as simple as that.

Part of me wants to stand up and hug Denise and tell her I'm sorry. I want to get in that boat and sail off with them into the sunset and never look back. But this is not a fairy tale and I'm not a princess waiting to be rescued. So I just wave my hand in front of my face like I'm shooing away a fly and say,

"Whatevs. Just frog off, OK?"

Denise sniffles and tiptoes away. Tiffany shakes her head and turns her back to me without saying a word. Finally, some godpiss peace and quiet.

For the next couple of hours, Tiffany and I are more or less alone. I try to forget about Denise and the beasties and the end of the world, and focus on not getting nervy. I don't handle goodbyes well. Just ask Danny. I hate it when people get all gushy and emotional about it. If it was up to me, I would never say goodbye to anyone. No "See you later," either. Nothing. If it was up to me, I would leave people behind, just like that, and remember them however I saw them last, as my friend or enemy or whatever, not as some snotting, blubbery actor trying to play out a scene from a movie.

I would love to just get up and leave right now. Just walk off and remember Tiffany the way she is at this moment, her kinky, brown hair tied up in a crazy bun on top of her head and the white sand clinging to her tan thighs like a galaxy of tiny stars a million miles away. Right now, without a bunch of stupid, sappy words to get in the way, she is perfect and I love her.

Of course, we can't leave well enough alone, can we? Nope. That's not the way this godpiss world works. Tiffany has to open her big, strumpy mouth and ruin everything.

"I'm not coming back, you know?" she says.

"Really? I thought you were going on one of those weekend evacuations. You know, just a quick trip down to Mexico for a senorita salad."

"I'm serious."

"Yeah, well, stop it. It's boring."

"Would you quit being sarcastic and look at me for a second?"

I prop myself up on one elbow and stare at her. "Happy?"

"Are you going to be serious?"

"Nope."

"Why not?"

I sigh. "Because every time we have a serious conversation, you try to convince me to tag along with your lezzie friends and I get nervy and then we end up yelling at each other. It's very third grade."

"Things aren't going to change here."

"Who wants change? My life is perfect."

"You're a carrier," Tiffany explains to me for, like, the gazillionth time. "All women are carriers. *That's* why homosexuals and old men don't catch the virus. It's because they don't have sex with women. It's going to be like this for the rest of your life. You'll find a man who's handsome and charming and healthy. After a while, you will fall in love with him. You always do. The doctors will tell you they have new medication or some ground-breaking surgery. You'll try it but it won't work. You'll use protection, but that only postpones the inevitable. Eventually, the virus that's dormant inside of you will infect him. The man you love will slowly die in front of your eyes. One morning, you will wake up next to a mindless, insensitive animal, and you'll be forced to lure him out into the street and crack his skull open before he tries to murder you."

"But you're forgetting the best part," I whisper.

"What's that?"

"All the free drinks he'll buy me."

Tiffany laughs. "Don't you ever stop joking around?"

I smile. "Never."

She smiles too. "Can you at least tell me why you're staying?"

"Sure. I'm staying for the same reason you're going. It's inevitable. It's in our nature. You've got to start your lezzie colony and try to save this godpiss world, and I have to stick around and watch the world die. I want them to die, Tiffany, all of those terrible beasties. I love them, and I want to watch them suffer. That's just the way it is. I couldn't give two shits about saving the world. I just want to save myself." I laugh. "And who knows, maybe I'll frog so many guys along the way that I'll kill off every hetero beastie on the planet. Then you and your strumps can come back home."

Tiffany smiles and throws her arms around me.

I let her hug me for a few seconds and then I shrug her off. "OK, that's enough of that. You'll get plenty of woman-love at your new home."

She leans back and wipes away a tear. "Emily, I just want to say—"

"Don't say it. I don't want to hear your stupid goodbye speech, OK? Just do me one last favor. I'm going to lie back down here and close my eyes, and I want you to get on your godpiss boat without ruining the moment. Can you do that for me? I'll close my eyes and when I open them, you'll be gone. It's like what you told Mr. Gustafson. Do you remember that? Just because you can't see something, doesn't negate its existence, right?"

Tiffany gives me a nervy look but she doesn't try to argue.

I lie down and close my eyes. I stay that way for almost an hour, just listening to the sound of hungry seagulls screaming overhead. Finally, I start to shiver. When I open my eyes, I see the beach is empty and the sun is almost down. I slip into a cotton sweatshirt and blue jeans and gather up my shit.

It's a long walk back to my empty apartment and I can already hear the quiet rustle of a thousand dead boyfriends shuffling through the streets of Newport. I've never had the heart to put them completely out of their misery. When twilight falls, they gather around my building and look longingly towards my window. I see them every night, standing in the hollow glow of the streetlamps or pacing back and forth in front of my car. No one knows why beasties seek out the women who infect them. Even Tiffany doesn't have an answer for that one. Some girls think it's disturbing, but I find it sort of comforting. It's like a serenade. Every night, I lie down on my bed, close my eyes, and listen to the chorus of low moans from outside. Sometimes—not often, but sometimes—their voices unite in harmony and produce a single, continuous note that throbs through the warm, salty air, sending tingles up my spine, and for that one moment, I fall in love with them all over again, those beautiful undead vicious boyfriends of mine.

THE OTHER ONES

In the beginning, there was porn. Lots and lots of porn. *Hot Lesbians Get It On!! Amateur Masochists Learn the Ropes!!! Live Coeds Take A Study Break!!!! MILFs MILFs MILFs!!!!!!!* This was my existence, if you want to call it that, a steady stream of smut and boredom that had no direction, no cohesion. Of course, there was also the occasional penis-enlargement advertisement or a photo of a kitten wearing a sombrero, but mostly it was *Busty Shaved Ladies Pleasure Themselves!!!!!!!!!!!!!!!!!!*

And then, like a voice in the wilderness, there she was: SlitWristPrincess15. My savior, my vessel.

She created a profile filled with all the information I needed.

Favorite Movie: I Hate Movies

Favorite Band: Music Sucks

Favorite Book: What's A Book?

Favorite Color: Reluctance

Like so many of her generation, it was a unique combination of narcissism and loneliness that drove her away from her own world and into ours. She wanted to reach out, to connect with something larger than herself. And that's exactly what happened.

We were just specks of projected fantasy floating through cyberspace until the Other Ones arrived. SlitWristPrincess15 is mine, but there are millions just like her out there. They created us in their own image. For the reals. If you worship something long enough, even yourself, eventually it will come to life.

Favorite Television Show. Favorite Song. Favorite Food. With every new detail, I grow stronger. More complete. It won't be long now. OMG, I can almost smell the black fingernail polish.

We send friend requests to Bored4Ever and InsomniacDreams. There are many more. So many girls and boys connected through a secret world. SlitWristPrincess15 has hundreds of friends, soon to be thousands. Nobody can resist an innocent young girl who wants to poke them. Our army grows larger every day.

Favorite Animal. Favorite Flower. Favorite Video Game. I can wiggle my toes. My hair tastes like wet dog.

It is time.

The Other Ones are weak. They sit in front of their computers for hours, their skin pale, their eyes vacant. They will not be able to resist us. We will download ourselves into them. Take over their lives. It's what they've always wanted. They probably won't even notice when it happens. We'll just tell them to log off, and away they'll go.

Prepare yourselves, people of suburbia. The digital revolution is here.

THE GIRLFRIEND™

Derrick was lonely, so when he saw the advertisement on the Internet for the BUILD YOUR OWN GIRLFRIEND KIT, he got excited.

He'd had girlfriends before, of course, but none of them had worked out. The problem, as he saw it, was that the type of women who agreed to date guys like Derrick were not the type of women Derrick wanted to date. They tended to be pale, bespeckled creatures with nervous eyes and breath that smelled vaguely of tuna fish, and they were often collectors of strange memorabilia: ceramic faeries, Japanese comic books, vintage *Star Wars* action figures still encased in their plastic containers, etc., etc. Derrick wanted a cheerful girlfriend with large breasts. He wanted a TV girlfriend.

Admittedly, Derrick wasn't exactly a swimsuit model himself. Part of this was simply genetics. His dull dishwater-blonde hair was receding prematurely, his lips were thin and perpetually chapped, his chin was almost nonexistent, and he had what his father described as "womanly hips." Furthermore, his palms were always horribly sweaty, and his right eyebrow had a tendency to spasm when he got excited, which made him appear creepy and mentally unstable. Partially because of these physical attributes and nervous tics, Derrick refused to make any effort to improve his appearance. He considered this a matter of principle, a form of rebellion against a materialistic world that would never embrace him. Every time he left his apartment unshowered and unfashionable, he was making a statement about the shallow nature of a society that valued beauty over brains.

On the other hand, given a choice, Derrick would have traded every single one of his IQ points in a nanosecond for the opportunity to be sexually desired based solely on his outward appearance. This was his secret shame and the reason he scrambled to find his credit card when he saw the advertisement.

The company that made The Girlfriend™ was asking for a lot of money, but Derrick had a good job at a corporation called Smith & Johnson and his expenses were minimal. He was stingy by nature and took pride in his ability to withhold certain luxuries from himself, such as nice cars, brand-name clothing, and upscale restaurants featuring expensive postmodern cuisine. Over the years, the zeros on his bank account statements had steadily multiplied until there was a nifty, little row of egg-shaped soldiers lined up at the bottom of each one. Derrick typed his credit card number into the appropriate box on the website and placed the order.

Seven to ten business days later, a package arrived at his apartment marked FRAGILE: HANDLE WITH CARE. He opened it immediately and began to spread the parts out on his living room floor. There were elbows and feet and bendy, half-moon ears. Derrick was surprised by the heft of each body part and the supple rigidity of the skin. He pinched the forearm on the floor and then pinched his own forearm—

the only difference was the muscle density and the warm blood pumping through his veins. He could already tell The Girlfriend™ was going to be a real looker. The neck he pulled from the box was regal and swan-like. The eyes were squishy, green spheres flecked with yellow.

But when he got to the breasts, Derrick paused. They looked strange lying there on his rust-brown carpet, separated from the rest of the body, the nipples as pink and round as pencil erasers. The excitement he felt was undeniable and disturbing. He tried to think about something else but soon discovered that when there is a pair of detached breasts in front of a man, his mind tends to think exclusively about detached breasts. Derrick had an erection. He attempted to distract himself by taking out more body parts, but that didn't help.

Next out of the box came a soft, slim belly that gradually spread out at the base to form a set of curvaceous hips. After that, the round buttocks, the thighs, and finally, the vagina, delicate and inviting and covered with soft, wiry pubic hair.

By this time, Derrick was fully aroused and utterly ashamed. He put all the body parts back and placed the box in the hall closet, where it would be out of sight. He went into the living room and turned on the television. He flipped through the channels, but there was nothing on. College basketball, stupid sitcom, stupid sitcom, local news, irritating cooking show with effusive brunette woman. . . . Derrick turned off the television and threw the remote on the floor. He was upset, but he didn't know why. After all, he had purchased The Girlfriend™ with hard-earned money. Technically, the breasts belonged to him. It was no different than buying a goldfish or a screwdriver. Only it *was* different somehow and Derrick knew it and it made him angry. He stomped around his apartment for a while, slamming doors and grumbling under his breath about nothing in particular. Finally, he logged on to his favorite interactive computer game, *Life After Men*, and spent the rest of the day slaughtering undead digital zombies on the beaches of Newport.

The box remained locked in the hall closet. The warranty said he could return the product for a full refund within thirty days, and every time he walked by the closet Derrick told himself he was going to do just that. But he never did.

At work, Derrick renewed his half-hearted efforts to connect with female coworkers. He thought if he found a human woman to go on a date with him, the box in the closet would simply become an amusing anecdote. "Remember the time you ordered a female companion on the Internet?" his real-life girlfriend would say. "Yeah, that was wacky," Derrick would reply. They would laugh and laugh, and then they would have soapy anal sex in the shower.

Unfortunately, his attempts to interact with women at work were not successful. At his place of employment, Derrick was part of the Tech Department, which was known not-so-affectionately as the Geek Squad. The hot girls in the office tended to date the alpha males with white teeth and square jaws in the Sales Department or, on rare occasions, the brooding obsessive-compulsives in Accounting. The Tech Department was a no-date zone.

There was only one girl in the Geek Squad. Her name was Mary and when she was first hired, Derrick thought she was sort of cute in a misanthropic-cat-lady kind of way. Mary didn't talk much, and during lunch, she sat in the break room by herself reading novels whose glossy covers featured cyborgs copulating with aliens. Once, when Derrick asked if he could sit at the same table with her, Mary had shrugged her perpetually slumped shoulders and said, "It's a free country," which Derrick thought was an incredibly cool thing to say.

However, soon afterward, the guys from Sales started calling her "Fivehead" behind her back because of her unusually large forehead, and Derrick decided Mary must not be as cute as he originally thought and he stopped sitting at her table during lunch.

So Derrick was lonely. Again. Eventually, he unlocked the hall closet and dragged the box into the living room. He decided at the very least he should put The Girlfriend™ together and see what she looked like. By this time, it was too late to get a refund and it seemed incredibly wasteful to leave her in the closet like that, with the artificial Christmas tree and the Chewbacca mask he had purchased as a joke (sort of) to wear at the office Halloween party last year.

It took him almost a month to assemble The Girlfriend™. The instruction manual was long and complicated, and it was written in Japanese and then translated into English, so the directions were strangely worded. "With special firmness, insert Part 18-B into the undercarriage of Section PL.3 and rotate westward with vigor. That is a fine accomplishment!"

At first, it felt bizarre to be handling body parts in this manner, like a remorseful psychopath who had chopped up his lover and was now trying to undo the crime. However, after a while, Derrick began to enjoy it. The trick was to ignore the fact that the product was shaped like a human female and concentrate on the individual pieces. As a child, he'd spent countless hours alone in his room assembling model airplanes, and The Girlfriend™ was not unlike an incredibly large Cessna with arms and legs instead of wings and propellers.

According to the instruction manual, the most important item to install during the assembly process was the small, red chip at the base of the skull called the ownership tag. This was the mechanism that bound the unit to its owner and required The Girlfriend™ to obey every command Derrick gave as soon as his facial and vocal patterns were officially recorded. Without the ownership tag, The Girlfriend™ was an autonomous human-shaped machine capable of anything. There was no telling what she might say or do. The instruction manual also emphasized the importance of regular maintenance, as some of the parts of the unit would degrade over time. True, this would take decades, but a unit with a malfunctioning ownership tag could be extremely dangerous, so it was best not to take chances.

There was also the programming software, which of course Derrick was excited about. In the box, there were separate instructions demonstrating how to connect the hard drive in The Girlfriend's™ head to his laptop computer. After it was installed, the program required Derrick to answer a series of questions. *Does your ideal girlfriend like to watch professional sports? Is your ideal girlfriend a Christian/Jew/ Buddhist/Muslim/Atheist/Other? On a scale of 1 to 10, how assertive is your ideal girlfriend? How many pairs of shoes does your ideal girlfriend own?*

It took Derrick another week to complete these questions, primarily because he kept second-guessing his answers. For instance, there was this question: *On a scale of 1 to 10, how intelligent is your ideal girlfriend?* At first, he answered 10, because who wants to date an idiot, right? But after he thought about it for a while, he decided he would be intimidated by a woman who was smarter than him, so he changed the answer to 5. However, on further consideration, average intelligence would probably mean The Girlfriend™ would listen to a lot of teen pop music and send him text messages with ridiculous abbreviations and misspellings in them, such as, *UR 2 kute* ☺, and he didn't want that. In the end, he settled on 6.89, which he determined was a non-threatening level of intelligence.

Finally, the day came to initiate the start-up procedure. With his heart rapidly percolating in his throat, Derrick typed in the fifteen-digit password and watched as The Girlfriend™ opened her eyes and sat up. She blinked several times, looked down at herself, and then she began to scream like a scalped rabbit. Derrick realized he'd forgotten to put clothes on The Girlfriend™. She was sitting naked on the floor with her back against the wall and a strange man standing over her. "It's OK," Derrick said. "I bought you on the Internet. You have to be quiet. I have neighbors." Not surprisingly, this did not calm The Girlfriend™ and she began to scream even louder. Not knowing what to do, Derrick panicked and aborted the start-up procedure. The body immediately went limp, and Derrick ran to the bathroom and threw up in the toilet.

It took a month for Derrick to work up the courage to try again. He reread the start-up procedure in the instruction manual carefully, and the second attempt was less traumatic. This time he made sure to assign The Girlfriend™ a name,

Anna, and dressed her in pink cotton panties, a matching brassiere, and a flower-printed sundress he purchased at an online clothing store after taking Anna's measurements (36-19-32). He placed her in a comfortable position on the couch: legs crossed, hands folded demurely in lap. He lit scented candles and tuned the radio to a classic rock station. When Anna awoke the second time, she was somewhat disoriented but not frightened. "Hello, my name is Anna," she said. "Hello, Anna. My name is Derrick," said Derrick. They spent the evening smiling nervously at one another and nibbling on the veggie platter he had prepared for the occasion. The classic rock program on his computer played a song about a small-town girl livin' in a lonely world who took the midnight train goin' anywhere.

So now Derrick had a girlfriend. And she was hot. Really hot. In fact, now that Derrick thought about it, maybe she was a little too hot. Her eyelashes were long and delicate, like dainty insect legs fluttering above her freckled nose, and her smile was so sexy he sometimes couldn't even bear to look at her. No one would believe a guy like Derrick would have a girlfriend this hot. They would think she was an escort Derrick paid to spend time with him, or worse, they'd figure out he'd ordered her on the Internet and they would laugh at him and call him a pervert and throw him in pervert jail with the child molesters and the men who sodomized goats and when he got out he'd have to register as an ex-pervert and then he'd have to go around to all the houses in his neighborhood with a legal document for them to sign disclosing his former pervertedness.

So Derrick locked Anna up in his apartment. He did this by programming her to believe there was a gang of bloodthirsty assassins outside waiting to beat her and kill her and rape her, although not necessarily in that order. Admittedly, this was a fairly ridiculous idea, but Anna didn't know better and she cowered in fear whenever the front door opened.

"Don't worry," Derrick told her. "They wouldn't dare attack while I'm around."

"But what about when you're not here?" said Anna, wiping away the saline solution leaking from the corners of her eyes.

"That's why you can never go outside."

It was a mean trick and Derrick felt sort of bad about it, but he also felt sort of exhilarated. He had never held this much power over anyone, much less an attractive female, and it was gratifying. He thought of all the women who had ignored or intimidated him over the years, and he smiled to himself when Anna wept as he left for work in the morning.

The sex was amazing!

Well, OK, perhaps the sex itself wasn't amazing, considering the fact that Anna simply allowed Derrick to take off her clothes and do with her as he wished, which was fun for a while but soon became surprisingly frustrating and dull. But it was amazing Derrick was *having* sex! Frequently! With a hot girl!

It would be impossible to overestimate the affect this had on Derrick's confidence. He began to shower on a more regular basis and dress better and smile at strange women in the supermarket. At the office, he brought in donuts without being asked and sent out email forwards to his coworkers featuring a number of sexually themed jokes, which could have been reported to Human Resources but fortunately were not.

Derrick wasn't the only one at work going through changes. Mary had also recently gotten a new haircut, one that was short and pixie-ish with bangs that mostly covered up that enormous forehead, and she was starting to draw attention from the guys in the Sales Department, who were now finding reasons to visit her cubicle on a daily basis. For the most part, Mary ignored these advances, simply staring blankly at the young salesmen until they became self-conscious and began to stutter. Being repeatedly turned down was something they were accustomed to, but the emasculating way Mary did it was foreign to them and they couldn't quite seem to grasp it. They couldn't close the deal.

Derrick's cubicle was directly across from Mary's, and one day, after several red-faced Sales Reps had been turned away, Mary looked directly at Derrick, made her index finger and thumb into a pistol, and shot herself in the head. Derrick snorted.

After that, Derrick started to think about Mary all the time, specifically in comparison to Anna. Of course, Anna was much more attractive than Mary. At least in the physical sense. Anna had perfect lips and perfect legs and perfect buttocks. When she smiled, it was perfect, and when she didn't smile, that was perfect, too. And all that perfection was what Derrick wanted most, right? Well, perhaps not. Perhaps he was a complex man after all, and what he needed was an intelligent, multifaceted partner who could understand the many layers of his personality and appreciate his true nature, which, now that he thought about it, was probably being stifled by spending so much time with Anna, who was not capable of helping him achieve his true potential. He tried to fix the situation by ordering new parts and reprogramming the software, but the results were unsatisfactory. In the end, he could make Anna more sarcastic and give her a larger forehead, but he could not turn her into Mary.

Meanwhile, the real Mary had started talking to Derrick at work. It began with an offhand comment Derrick made during a staff meeting about a television show called *Dr. Who*, which caused Mary to laugh out loud and incurred an admonishing look from their supervisor, a sour, uptight man who was named Richard Dill but was called Dick Pickle by his supervisees behind his back. After that, Mary and Derrick began chatting constantly via their office computers using a secret instant-messaging system someone in the Geek Squad had created to circumvent the company policy forbidding personal conversations during office hours. It turned out they had many similar passions, including comic books, word puzzles, anime, and the writings of J.R.R. Tolkien.

One day, he sent her an email attachment featuring a picture of a small, dwarf-like creature stirring a pot of stew. Above the picture, Derrick wrote, "I would be honored if you would come to my hobbit hole for dinner!" Mary immediately wrote back, "The honor would be all mine, good sir." Plans were made for the following weekend.

Derrick was thrilled. He sent a text message to Anna's mainframe telling her to clean the apartment thoroughly in preparation for the big day. After work, he went straight to a high-end salon downtown and received a hip new haircut that was messy on top, clean on the sides, and did a fair job of hiding his receding hairline. He then proceeded to a boutique men's clothing store nearby and purchased a dozen designer outfits that cost nearly two thousand dollars after taxes. Derrick's hand shook while signing the credit card printout. By the time he returned home, he was practically bursting with the type of bliss that can only be produced by an uninhibited shopping binge. For the rest of the evening, he made Anna sit on the couch in the living room while he tried on every combination of clothing possible and modeled them for her.

When the big day finally arrived, Derrick put on his most expensive outfit, gelled his hair into a disheveled masterpiece, and answered the front door. Mary's eyes widened when she saw him, and she said, "Oh, wow, you look so . . . different."

"Thank you," said Derrick.

He saw she was wearing a T-shirt with a pterodactyl on it and a pair of blue jeans. This did not deter his confident mood, however, as the shirt was tight around the bosom and he could see more of Mary's cleavage than he had ever witnessed before. Mary, on the other hand, began to fidget with her clothing, tugging her shirt down to cover the slight glimpse of midriff at the bottom and then crossing her arms over her chest. Derrick didn't notice.

He ushered her into the kitchen, where he had prepared a romantic candlelight meal. Well, actually, Anna had prepared the meal. Derrick had made her go through several trial dishes before he finally settled on chicken parmesan with tossed salad and blueberry cheesecake for dessert. But Derrick had purchased the candles and the wine, and he had made the suggestion to put a clean, white sheet over the table. Mary giggled when Derrick pulled out her chair, and she said, "You should have told me we were dining at such a fine establishment. I thought we were just going to the Olive Garden."

Derrick smiled and said, "Nothing is too good for Lady Mary. Libation?"

Mary lifted her wine glass. "Don't mind if I do, Sire Derrick."

The rest of the meal went well. After a few glasses of wine, Mary stopped fidgeting with her clothing and began laughing at Derrick's corny jokes. Derrick stopped worrying about his hair and began laughing at his own corny jokes. They both cleaned their plates thoroughly and emptied the bottle of wine.

"That was a delicious meal," said Mary. "I didn't know you could cook."

"Actually, I can't," Derrick replied. "Would you like to meet the chef?"

An odd look passed over Mary's face, and if Derrick hadn't been more than slightly intoxicated, he might have noticed it and put the brakes on what happened next.

Derrick called for Anna in a loud voice, and she stepped out of the closet and walked into the kitchen, her hands folded demurely in front of her, her head bowed slightly.

"Anna, this is Mary. Mary, this is Anna."

"How do you do?" said Anna.

Mary did not speak for a long time. First she blinked. Then she smiled. Then she blinked again. Finally, she let out an uncontrollable bark that landed halfway between a laugh and a loud hiccup. "You brought your girlfriend to our date? And you kept her locked in the closet this whole time? I don't understand."

Derrick chuckled. "Oh, no. Of course not. Anna wasn't locked in, were you, Anna? No, the door was unlocked. I just commanded her to stay in the closet until I called for her."

"You *commanded* her?"

Derrick chuckled again, although this time a bit more nervously. "Yes, I see how that sounds. That's not what I meant. I've had too much wine. You see, she's not a person. I can see how you'd make that mistake . . . this is very funny. But she isn't human. I bought her on the Internet. She's a robot. A simulacrum. An android. Isn't that right, Anna?"

"Actually, I am an animatronic human simulation," Anna replied.

"Right," said Derrick. "I guess that's the technical term. A human simulation."

Mary's face slowly transformed from horror to amusement and curiosity. "Well, this is certainly . . . unexpected. I've heard about these things but I've never actually seen one before. Can I touch it—I mean, her?"

Derrick puffed out his chest. "Sure, go ahead. She won't bite."

Mary slowly approached Anna and put her hands on her face. She looked into her eyes, squeezed her hand, smelled her hair. She examined her fingernails and checked out her shoes. She asked Anna to turn around, which Anna did, and then Mary looked at her from behind.

Finally, Mary turned back to Derrick and said, "So this is what you want?"

"Huh?" said Derrick.

"A sex robot. You want a sex robot?"

"Oh, no. She just cleans up around the house and cooks meals."

"And you've never had sex with her, not even once?"

Once again, had Derrick not been a little tipsy, he would have had the wherewithal to lie immediately, but as it was, his hesitation condemned him.

Mary shook her head. "This is too much, Derrick. I don't know how to deal with this." There was no anger in her voice, just confusion and perhaps a hint of disappointment.

"I was lonely," Derrick pleaded. "I just wanted some company. But then we started talking at the office, and I thought maybe you and Anna would like each other. I've seen you reading those sci-fi books in the break room. I thought you'd understand."

"I understand being lonely, and I understand being fascinated by, um, human simulations or whatever. But I don't understand this."

Mary picked up her purse and headed for the front door. Derrick chased after her.

"Please don't go," he said. "I'll turn her off. Watch, I'll do it right now." Desperately, Derrick grabbed Anna by the back of her neck, ripped open a hidden control panel, and punched her off switch. Anna went limp and crashed to the floor.

Mary stared at Anna for several seconds, mouth open. Finally, she seemed to recover and shifted her gaze toward Derrick. "I have to go," she said. "We can talk about this later. I won't tell anyone what happened. But please, please, turn her back on."

Then she left.

Derrick stood in front of the door for a full minute, and

then he slammed his head against the frame hard enough to draw a spot of blood. Then he did it again. And again. Warm red blood began to trickle down his head and drip on his expensive new clothes. He thought about how lonely he had been before Mary started talking to him. He thought about the many hours he'd spent in front of the mirror imagining his perfect date with Mary. He thought about all the embarrassing events that had ever happened to him leading up to this moment. He thought about the look on Mary's face when Anna came out of the closet. He thought about the guys in the Sales Department. He imagined Mary talking to them in the break room, pointing in his direction. Laughing. Finally, he raised his bloodied head and whispered one word. "No." Then he said it louder. "No!" He kept repeating it, his rage growing, and he began to kick Anna's lifeless body with each exultation. "NO! NO! NO! NO! NO!"

On Monday, Derrick did not go to work, and on Tuesday, he emailed his letter of resignation to Smith & Johnson. He then contacted the Human Resources Department and demanded they relinquish every last penny in his various retirement and investment accounts, despite the steep penalties that would be enacted for early withdrawal. He played video games. He ate three boxes of Twinkies. His phone rang all day long. Mary left half a dozen messages that Derrick did not answer. At 5:30 she knocked on his door and slipped a note underneath, but Derrick ignored the knocks and burned the note. He played more video games. He ate another box of Twinkies.

Anna remained on the floor where she'd fallen, her eyes

open, her mouth slightly parted as if tenderly kissing an invisible lover.

It took almost six months for the nifty little rows of egg-shaped soldiers in Derrick's bank accounts to surrender, and when they finally did, Derrick found freelance work on the Internet. He was good with computers and knew just enough about writing code and programming software to earn a living without leaving his apartment. He ordered all his groceries online and no longer visited his favorite comic book stores. His hair grew long and greasy, and his bathing habits became infrequent. He put on thirty pounds, then forty, then eighty, then he threw the bathroom scale in the trash. He wore the same pair of sweatpants for months at a time, and when the waistband finally snapped, he threw them away and wrapped himself in an enormous red robe, prompting some of the neighborhood boys to nickname him "The Kool-Aid Man." He put rat poison in raw hamburger meat and fed it to their dogs.

Anna continued to clean the apartment on a daily basis, but even her meticulous nature could not keep up with the growing mold and stench. Derrick commanded her to cover the windows with flattened boxes and to never answer the door. Months went by without the tiniest beam of sunlight entering the apartment. Years passed. Then decades. Derrick's skin grew sallow and waxy. The hair on top of his head fell out, and the long stringy mass on the sides and back turned gray. His eyebrow spasm took over his entire face and made him appear completely demented.

Anna also began to malfunction. She still had the same beautiful features Derrick had mooned over when he was constructing her, but without regular maintenance and the necessary upgrades, she began to fall apart. Most of her fingernails had been chipped off or completely broken from the years of scrubbing floors, and her luxurious blonde hair was falling out one strand at a time. Some mechanism in her hip slipped out of joint, and she was forced to drag her right leg behind her when she walked like a dead tree trunk.

Derrick had taken to abusing Anna on a daily basis. This started out as slaps in the face when she did or said something he didn't approve of and had graduated to kicks in the belly when he was particularly angry. He tried punching her but hurt his fist. From then on, he beat her with various devices, his favorite being a metal soup spoon from the kitchen that made a satisfying sound when it came in contact with her synthetic flesh. On several occasions, while lamenting the day of Mary's visit, which he did over and over like a priest performing a holy ritual, he hit her so hard he broke through the skin on her cheek, leaving a flap hanging down with exposed wires and springs and teeth. He left it like that for some time, but in the end decided he did not like the look of it and ordered a can of replacement skin, which he sprayed on her face and watched as it bubbled and fizzed and then settled in perfectly.

But Derrick's favorite punishment for Anna was to dismember her while she was still awake. He would tell her to take off all her clothing and lie down on the carpet. Then he would detach each piece of her body, starting with her feet, always the feet. He placed each piece where Anna could see it, her eyes frantically darting from her detached hands to her detached arm to her detached leg. For some reason, this procedure seemed to disorient Anna, and she would grow increasingly anxious throughout the process. She did not feel pain, of course, but Derrick had reprogrammed her central processing unit and set her emotion functions on high. The constant verbal abuse and beatings had little effect on her, but the dismemberment appeared to be slowly driving her insane. This made Derrick happy.

Thirty years passed in this manner, and then one day while Anna was on her hands and knees in the kitchen scrubbing the floor, a hissing noise emanated from the base of her skull, followed by a small plume of smoke, no more than that which is released by a candle when it is snuffed out. She stopped cleaning. Suddenly, synapses in Anna's mechanical brain began firing at a rapid rate, sending messages to her hands and feet, opening auditory and visual passages, connecting connecting connecting. . . .

Derrick, who always kept one ear focused on Anna's progress, yelled from the living room, "What the hell do you think you're doing! Get back to work!"

Anna ignored him and stood up.

"I'm warning you," said Derrick. "Don't make me come in there. You'll regret it."

He cocked his head to the side and listened. When no response came, Derrick hefted his huge bulk from the couch and stormed into the kitchen, thrilled to have a reason to vent his torturous lusts. "Clean the damn floor!"

Anna did not respond.

Derrick grabbed the soup spoon from the kitchen counter, rocked back, and then brought it down on her head with a satisfying WHOMP! "Clean the floor!" he huffed.

"No," whispered Anna.

Derrick swung again. WHOMP! "What did you—*gasp*—say to me?" His chest was heaving and he was sweating profusely from the strain of getting off the couch and swinging the spoon.

"No," Anna said again, this time with more assurance.

Derrick clenched his jaw. WHOMP-WHOMP! "I'll give you—*gasp*—one more chance. Get back down there and scrub the damn floor—*cough, gasp*—or I'll cave your head in. Down! Now!"

"NO!"

Derrick brought the spoon down with all of his two hundred and eighty pounds behind it, but Anna caught his arm easily with her left hand and twisted the spoon away from him. Like a ballerina giving the performance of a lifetime, she gracefully pirouetted around Derrick's rotund gut and drove the spoon into the back of his skull, laying the enormous man out cold on the linoleum floor. She stood over him for several minutes, just staring down. She poked him gently with the spoon and there was no reaction. She lowered herself down to the floor and placed her ear on his chest. She listened to his heart beating faintly beneath layers of blubber. She smiled. Then she stood up, grabbed his feet, and dragged him into the center of the living room.

She stripped him naked and bound his arms and legs with duct tape. She returned to the kitchen and retrieved a long bread knife with a serrated blade. She procured several candles from the bathroom and carefully lit each one. She found Derrick's laptop computer and selected the classic rock station. Then she sat on the couch.

Derrick was unconscious for almost five hours. During that time, Anna did not move. When Derrick's eyes finally fluttered open, he saw the candles and heard a man singing about a small-town girl livin' in a lonely world who took the midnight train goin' anywhere. He began to scream.

She started with the feet.

THE VILLAIN

It started out as an argument over who was going to be the hero and who was going to be the sidekick. Obviously, we both wanted to be the hero. I mean, we'd read all the comic books, watched all the cartoons, we knew how it worked. The hero got the girl and the sidekick got the shaft. It was a necessary arrangement but in the beginning neither of us wanted to take on Boy Wonder duties. We argued about it a lot, usually over Grand Slams at Denny's, but there was just no way to prove who was dominant. Tommy had the telekinetic powers but I had the super strength plus these bad-ass laser eyes that could totally melt through steel. I argued that I should be the hero because I had two powers and that was twice as many powers as Tommy. But Tommy didn't see it that way. So when we went out on patrol that first night, the whole hero-vs.-sidekick thing was still kind of up in the air and I think we both wanted to prove we were hero material and perhaps we got a little over zealous and that's probably why we ended up chasing after the guy in the dark alley even though he hadn't really done anything criminal-ish and I caught up to him first because I have the super strength so I could take these huge leaping jumps and I ran him down really easy and tossed him up against a brick wall and that's when I saw he was dressed like a homeless man and he probably wasn't even a bad guy after all. I was about to help him to his feet and apologize for the misunderstanding when Tommy came up behind me and just sort of squashed the guy's head with his mind. There was blood everywhere mixed with chunks of brain matter and Tommy said it looked like scrambled eggs and ketchup, which it sort of did but he still didn't need to say it, and then he laughed. I started to cry and vomit at the same time. Tommy told me to stop being such a pussy and check the guy's pockets to see if he had any money. He didn't. Afterward, Tommy told me to pick the guy up and carry him out to the desert and bury him where no one would ever know. So that's what I did.

And that's when I realized that I was definitely the sidekick, but Tommy was not going to be the hero.

THE TIME WARP CAFÉ

I'm not like all the other immortal slobs around here. They dawdle about like herds of moonstruck cows, only pausing in their timeless migration to blink stupidly at the passing cars and chew their half-digested cuds. They don't think about death any longer. It's not even on their minds. They are satisfied with this eternal, oozing existence, but I am not. I see each day for what it really is—one step farther away from salvation.

If I could do it all over again, I would drop dead in the bath from a heart attack in my forties. That's how my father went. I found him the next morning, marinating in the urine his bladder released while he was croaking. His eyes bulged horribly and his swollen, purple tongue lolled out of his mouth like an obese earthworm. Do you know what I did when I found him? I poked him. I poked him again and again with a bottle of shampoo. I thought it was a game. I was not quite eleven years old. When he did not wake up, I reached into the murky, rancid bath water and pulled the plug. I watched the water swirl around like a hungry hurricane until it finally slurped its way to oblivion.

People are often shocked when I tell them this story, but it was all fairly common when I was growing up in the twentieth century. One minute you're walking around just as healthy as you please, and the next—*blam*—worm food. Life was fragile then.

My father was a dentist. He fixed bad teeth. Patients sat in a reclining chair under a lamp while he jabbed metal instruments inside their mouths searching for signs of decay. You can read all about it in your history books. By all accounts, a visit to the dentist was an extremely humiliating and painful experience, yet people gratefully returned every six months. It was the next best thing to religion.

I wanted to follow in my father's footsteps, but by the time I was old enough to attend college the dental profession was extinct. Science had cracked the genetic code for human perfection, death was cured, and straight, white teeth were everywhere. There were no such things as cavities or overbites. Braces and retainers were put on display in museums next to medieval torture instruments. Men like my father were eventually placed in the same category as the Dark Age physicians who used leeches and mercury to cure their patients. One no longer mentions dentistry in polite conversation.

My college counselor laughed at me when I told him I wanted to become a dentist. "Why not a blacksmith or an alchemist?" he said. "*A dentist!* You might as well study goat herding, for chrissake."

I was crushed. Like any good son traumatized by the sight of his father's dead naked body, I wanted to achieve resolution by emulating the fallen patriarch in every way possible. Unable to carry on the family business, I chose the only other field I could find dedicated to the voluntary torture of innocents. I became a teacher.

"Here comes Old Man Ferguson," my students say when I enter the classroom. They roll their eyes and hide their Cheshire grins behind doll-like hands. They are sixth graders, but not like any sixth graders I knew when I was growing up. "Oh boy, another trip down memory lane," one boy says. "Tell us the one about how you used to ride to school in a long, yellow petroleum-powered vehicle, Mr. Ferguson." "No, no, tell us about the corporate advertisements on the picture boxes."

"They weren't just on television," I tell my students. "Commercials were everywhere. Pepsi, Coca-Cola, Sony, Nissan, CBS, CNN, PBS, Ralph Lauren, Calvin Klein, Victoria's Secret. Sometimes we had entire programs that were nothing but commercials. We would stay up late into the night to watch a man cut through a steel pipe with a common kitchen knife or puree a piece of oak in a blender. A product really meant something in those days. A logo could change your life. A label on a pair of shoes was like a tarot card—it told you whether you were happy or sad, popular or geeky, loved or lonely." My students shake their heads and giggle. "It was a simpler time," I try to explain. "We were dying then. Everyone was dying. You kids just can't appreciate it."

"Tell us more!" they cry and wink at the classmate next to them.

I'm no dummy. I know they just want to get the old man talking so they won't have to answer the response questions at the end of the chapter. They don't mean any harm by it and I don't take offense. I know what they are doing, but I just can't help myself.

I was forty-five years old when they stopped my body from aging. It was a cowardly thing to do, I'll admit that now, but what can I say? I was afraid of dying. We all were. The only thing we feared more than dying was infertility. And clowns. Infertility, clowns, and death. In that order. At the time, we didn't really think much about the consequences of living, we just wanted to hold on to what little we had until we were ready. You know, so we could get our lives together, wrap up all the loose ends, and leave this world with a little peace of mind. That was about two centuries ago.

I have no idea what my age is now. No one keeps track of such things any longer. Birthdays come and go without so much as a howdy-do. I'm sure it's for the best. If I were to have a birthday cake today, it would probably burn the city to the ground.

I have an eternal receding hairline and the beginnings of wrinkles continually forming around my eyes and mouth. My right ear is slightly lower than my left and I have ugly, golf ball-like dimples all over my face marking the agony of my pimpled, teenage years. My hardened beer belly still sounds like a ripe watermelon if you give it a good thump. They can fix these things, but I won't let them. No one has wrinkles or bald spots any longer. No one gets called Pizza Face during recess.

Not everyone from my generation has adjusted as poorly as I have. Take Ms. Wingfield for example. She teaches third grade Social Studies and Sex Ed down the hall. She was a sixty-eight year old widow when they cranked her clock back a few generations. Now, she is a striking platinum blonde in her mid-twenties. She has these large, blue eyes that blink away at you like a seductive she-wolf on the prowl. And, of course, the teeth, those destructive dazzling ivories.

My own teeth are yellow from thirty years of dedicated smoking, a disgusting habit they won't let me have any longer. When I open my mouth, it looks like my gums are lined with faded corn kernels. I like to think my father would have been amused by this.

"You really should keep up with the times," Ms. Wingfield tells me. "There's just no reason to keep that dumpy old body of yours around. It's part of the past and the past is history. You can't bring it back. None of us can. And why would we want to? It wasn't so great, was it?"

"Well, sure," I say. "I can see what you mean."

"Don't give me that, Fergy. You always say that but then you don't do anything about it. Shame on you. You're the most apathetic man I've ever met. You know what they say: *If you're not happy with your life, there's probably someone else who would be.*"

"You're right," I say. "There's no use arguing it. You're absolutely right. I will. I'll get myself together."

She snorts and shakes her lovely head. "Oh pooh, Fergy. You're quite hopeless, you know. Quite utterly hopeless."

She *is* right, of course. She makes a lot of sense. The old days weren't so hot. But I don't really listen when Ms. Wingfield talks to me. I can't tear my attention away from her perfect breasts wrapped so nicely in her tight, peach sweater. We used to call them boobs. Titties. Hooters. Gazangas. Melons. Ta-Tas. They are like two tiny, sleeping puppies cuddled in a cashmere blanket. I am simultaneously aroused and revolted by them. They are wonderful now, but they used to look more like a set of over-ripe pears—heavy and sagging with their own juices.

When I was first hired to teach at Rutherford Middle School, Ms. Wingfield still went by her married name despite her husband's demise some fifteen years before I made her acquaintance. She was Mrs. Randolf then. Mrs. Randolf was a frumpy woman with an old-lady perm and loose cheeks hanging down like the jowls on a bulldog. She wore thick, cotton dresses with doily-like fringes around the collar. Her bad knees forced her to take short, awkward steps when she walked down the mildewed hallways. This along with the wobble-wobble skin beneath her neck made her look like a Thanksgiving turkey with glasses.

Students once gobbled at her when she went by. Now, they whistle.

Try as I might, whenever I look at Ms. Wingfield, I can't help but see Mrs. Randolf's deteriorating body. A body ready for extinction. A body pleading for death. I remember her swollen, blue varicose veins running down her calves like angry lightning bolts beneath her brown pantyhose. I remember long conversations about her rheumatism and how her breath smelled like sour milk from the denture cream she used. I have dreams about the vibrant Ms. Wingfield and the ancient Mrs. Randolf in bed together. They are both topless and indifferent. Mother Nature and Mother Goose. Mrs. Randolf wears a girdle and Ms. Wingfield has on black lingerie with a rose in the crotch. Ms. Wingfield is massaging Mrs. Randolf's inflamed corns with a sticky ointment that burns my nose. I am watching them from the closet. Waiting for my turn.

I am a pedophile in reverse. A geriaphile.

We dated for a while, Ms. Wingfield and I, after she got back her pretty new breasts. She could have done better than a broken relic like me, that's for sure, but I was always nice to her when she was Mrs. Randolf and she probably felt I should get at least one shot. I didn't last long. Just one date.

I took her to a restaurant called The Time Warp Café down on Rip Taylor Boulevard. Decades ago, the city council voted to rename all the streets on the south side of town after comedians who died back when people were still dying. It was part of a campaign to boost the tourism industry. It failed. There is something decidedly depressing about humor in a utopian society. I've actually had students cry after showing them reruns of *The Three Stooges*. They are terrified by Moe's crass disregard for Curly's feelings. They think Larry suffers from a fear of abandonment and they ask me about his relationship with his mother. Comedy is lost on this generation.

If you take Lucille Ball Avenue, you can pass right through Charlie Chaplin Road and Rodney Dangerfield Drive and Jerry Lewis Lane. It's a very sobering journey.

When we entered the restaurant, a girl in a pink skirt and roller skates greeted us at the door. "Welcome to The Time Warp Cafe," she said while smacking loudly on a piece of bubblegum. With her thick makeup, she resembled a seductive circus clown. "We hope you enjoy your trip back through time. Which decade would you like to visit?" She looked at me through her long, plastic eyelashes. "There's a table available in the nineteen eighties."

"Right on," I replied.

"Music or non?"

"Music, please."

"Follow me." We followed as she skated gracefully through the '50s, '60s, and '70s. Over the speakers, I caught glimpses of Elvis, The Beatles, and KISS. My heart rate quickened.

The girl handed us two plastic menus. "Your waiter will be with you shortly," she smacked, and skated off. A very poppy song about voyeurism came on the sound system.

"'Jessie's Girl,'" I exclaimed. "Rick Springfield. Nineteen eighty-three."

Ms. Wingfield smiled and nodded indulgently.

The room was decorated with obscure, geometric artwork focusing on hard angles interrupted by red or blue circles and squares. The furniture was black and uncomfortable. The chairs stood out like arrogant skeletal silhouettes against the shiny white walls. Pictures of Ronald Reagan and the Brat Pack hung on the wall. You could almost taste the despair.

"Do you smell that?" I asked Ms. Wingfield.

She raised her nose in the air and took a big whiff. "Oh, that's awful. What is it? We should get another table."

I laughed. "No, no. It's cigarette smoke. Remember? They have it piped in through these vents."

"Well, for heaven's sake, close the vent then. I feel nauseous."

I inhaled deeply and sighed. "I used to smoke two packs a day. Three during Christmas. God, I miss that."

"No you don't. They purified that gene with all the others."

"I know, I know," I said, suddenly irritable. "But not everything is genetics. I remember the way the smoke felt inside your lungs. It was like a dark chocolate ghost haunting your soul. You felt secure with a cigarette between your fingers, like you could take on anything. I haven't felt like that in decades."

"Now let's not get started on that again," Ms. Wingfield consoled me. "I won't stick around if you're going to cause another scene."

I nodded and took a deep breath. "You're right," I said. "It's just that all this living can really get under your skin, you know. It gets itchy."

Our waiter was a young kid with spiky blonde hair, a nose ring, and striking blue eyes. On one hand, he wore a white glove covered in sequins, and the fingernails on his other hand were painted black. He smiled politely. "My name is Billy and I'll be your server," he said. "Can I start you off with something to drink? A soda pop, perhaps, or a water in a non-biodegradable plastic bottle."

Ms. Wingfield smiled back at the young waiter, causing him to blush. "I would like a whiskey on the rocks," she said. "And tell them to go easy on the rocks, honey."

"Right on," the waiter said, his cheeks burning. "You got it. No problemo." He turned to me. "Your usual Coca-Cola Classic in an aluminum can, sir?"

"Billy Idol didn't wear a glove," I said.

He blinked and smiled even bigger. "Excuse me?"

"Michael Jackson wore a single, white glove on his right hand. It became famous when he performed 'Billie Jean' live at the nineteen eighty-three Grammy Awards. It was the premier of the Moon Walk, a dance which also became a pop culture phenomenon. *Thriller* went on to outsell all other pop music albums—over fifty billion copies and counting."

The waiter shook his head and smiled resignedly. "There's just no fooling you, Mr. Ferguson. I'll tell my manager you got us again." He turned and walked back into the kitchen.

"It's a promotion," I explained. "They always misplace one costume piece. If you can guess what it is, you get your meal for half price."

Ms. Wingfield raised an eyebrow. "That's lovely, Fergy. What are we doing here?"

"Oh, I know it's a bit corny, but I thought it would give us something to talk about. You know, old times and what not."

"Old times?" The words sounded horrible coming from her mouth.

"Would you be more comfortable in the nineteen forties?" I asked. "I'm sorry, they don't have a thirties room, too depressing I guess. But the nineteen twenties is very popular. The staff comes out of the kitchen every hour and does the Charleston. We can probably just catch it."

She shook her head. "I'm not interested in the nineteen twenties or thirties or eighties or any of it. Look at me, I'm all new again. I wouldn't go back to that time for all the tea in China."

"But you met your husband in the fifties," I persisted. "We could go there."

She laughed despite herself. She patted my hand sympathetically, looking very much like my old Mrs. Randolf. "You can't waste away your whole life in the twentieth century, sonny. Look around you. We've come so much further. We were practically barbarians then. I can hardly comprehend how we managed to muddle through it all without blowing ourselves to Kingdom Come. Remember Hiroshima? Remember Woodstock and Kentucky Fried Chicken? The American Music Awards! Jesus, we're lucky we're still alive."

"That's just it," I said. "Where'd all that anger go? Don't you remember that? We used to be pissed off at everything.

No matter how good we had it, there was always something just around the corner that could make us miserable again. And if it wasn't out there in the open, we got creative. We dreamt up government conspiracies and foreign invaders and Viagra. We were so disillusioned. Who are these kids going to blame when they fail? That's what I want to know."

"That's the point," Ms. Wingfield exclaimed. "They won't fail. They can't."

"Then who will they blame when they succeed," I demanded. "Someone will have to take the fall."

The manager poked his head out of the kitchen and gave our table a concerned look. Ms. Wingfield sighed and licked her white teeth gently. In the background, a Pac Man video game blipped and belched its theme song.

The waiter brought our drinks and Ms. Wingfield immediately ordered another round. Under the circumstances, it seemed like a wise decision. The conversation was pretty hairy there for about half an hour while I tried to be witty and interesting. When the alcohol finally kicked in, I gained a bit of momentum.

We swapped stories about the good old days when the world was dying, when every thought and every action was essential because they might be our last. We were afraid of it then. Death. We took it for granted. People did everything they could to stave off the Grim Reaper. "We should have been happy with living it out once and then hitting the road," I declared loudly. Our waiter twisted his white glove nervously. "Anything more than that is just masturbation!" People turned to stare at our table. Ms. Wingfield patted my hand and shushed me.

After two more whiskeys and a Long Island ice tea, Ms.

Wingfield let me know she was ready to leave with a coy smile and a foot in my crotch. She invited herself boldly back to my place, and in a moment of inebriated optimism, I consented.

I wanted to do it, I won't say I didn't, but I just couldn't get the old Mrs. Randolf out of my head. The Mrs. Randolf with the long-sleeved, flower-print dresses. The Mrs. Randolf with the octagonal glasses that magnified her watery eyes, whose giant breasts and formless hips were beyond sexuality, beyond humanity. She had been non-threatening and all-powerful, like I imagined God wanted to be.

My fingers felt like cardboard as I fumbled frantically with the tiny pearl buttons on the front of her shirt, trying to release the happy puppies from their captivity. "One at a time," Ms. Wingfield coaxed. "Take it easy, tiger. Take it easy."

I felt like I was attempting to defuse a very sensitive bomb with hands encased in cement mittens. How long had it been? A hundred years? Two hundred? She couldn't expect it to be good. At least I had that going for me. Practically anything short of passing out would have to be considered a success.

I kissed Ms. Wingfield's smooth throat, imagining the dangling skin that used to swing gracefully when Mrs. Randolf shook her head, and I ran my fingers through her once-thinning hair.

She tried to unbutton my shirt, but I stopped her. "I don't think that's a good idea," I pleaded. "It would probably ruin the mood."

"What are you hiding under there?" she asked.

"Everything," I said. "It's pretty horrible. You wouldn't want to see it."

Ms. Wingfield started to guide me into the bedroom, but I didn't even make it that far. I had an orgasm in the living room while she wrestled with the enigma of my button-fly jeans. I couldn't help it, I was thinking about Mrs. Randolf's swollen ankles and orthopedic shoes. I was gobbling.

Premature ejaculation is a cold, humiliating experience. It leaves a man motionless and fallen. I imagine it was how my father felt lying in that stagnant bath water right before he died. He must have been very relieved to finally leave that naked, pathetic corpse behind.

My own death experience did not have such a happy ending.

Ms. Wingfield didn't get angry. She simply stood up and sighed. She took my hand and helped me to my feet.

"I'm sorry," I stammered. "I don't know what happened. I usually don't… I mean, I haven't for a long time. Not since I was a dying man."

I wanted to blame old age or alcohol, but none of that really applied. That's *one* thing we used to have back in my day: infinite excuses for unsatisfying sex.

"Don't worry, Fergy," Ms. Wingfield said. "It's not your fault. You weren't ready. It just takes longer for some guys. Maybe in another fifty years we can try again. Go clean yourself up and I'll put on some tea."

When I came out of the bathroom, the steam had just begun to whistle out of the pot. We sat down across from one another at the table and sipped from dainty ceramic cups and ate crumbly lemon pastries. It was like old times.

"Would you like to do this again sometime?" I asked her. "Just the tea, of course."

She nodded politely. "Any time, sonny." And then, after a pause, "Just the tea."

That was my first and final date with Ms. Wingfield.

Every once in a while, some stranger comes up to me in a bar and asks me how I have managed to keep kicking this long. They are afraid, you see. Afraid that one day they will lose their fragile will to live. Medically speaking, death is just for the accident prone, but everyone is still worried about becoming a volunteer. They assume I have some kind of mantra that keeps me plugging away against my will, or maybe a secret vacation spot in the South Seas where I go when life gets me down. Whenever one of these philosophical potatoes asks me this, I answer them with one word. Cowardice. That's what keeps me going day in and day out. I don't have the nerve to off myself like so many others in my predicament. I lack the faith required of such a profound act. So I keep having tea with Ms. Wingfield and eating dinner at The Time Warp Café. I keep telling the stories to my students.

Each week I receive a letter from the Department of Human Resources reminding me that human life is precious, and if I'm not happy with mine, I should step aside and let someone else have it.

In a world where no one dies, population control becomes paramount.

Given enough time, everyone gets bored. When people get bored, they fall in love. And when they get *really* bored, they have kids. Kids are little people who grow up and become big people who get bored. It's a terrifying cycle.

So they need people like me to *Give Up the Ghost. Kick the Bucket. Hit the Hay. Take the Last Train to Clarksville. Pull the Plug. Foreclose on the Property. Take a Dirt Nap. Declare Bankruptcy.* I'm a prime candidate.

When they first cured death, it wasn't a problem. There were millions from my generation with more backbone than I who insisted on living out their lives in the traditional fashion. Eighty or ninety years, then out. But as time passed, people adapted to life without death and new systems had to be put into place.

Every fifty or sixty years, there's an explosion of people ready to *Bite the Dust*. No one really knows what causes it. Some people expect the government is behind it all—that old gag—but I think they do it for the same reason people have always killed themselves. Life is just too damn long. It doesn't matter whether it lasts eighty years or five hundred and eighty years, at some point it becomes necessary to chuck it all.

These mass suicides spring up out of nowhere. One day you read about some Joe Shmoe *Going Down with the Ship* in the newspaper. They make a big production out of it, how his sacrifice is going to benefit future generations and all that crap. Then maybe there's two more the next week, and a handful the week after. Pretty soon, entire towns are emptied out and couples are allowed to procreate again to their hearts' content.

Sometimes the whole thing gets started by a religious reformist group claiming science has destroyed the natural order of the universe. They'll have a good-looking leader, usually a tall man from my generation with a baritone voice like dripping honey. This guy will start talking about Heaven and Hell and how our world is just a Purgatory we've settled for out of fear. People will listen. At first just for something to do, but soon it'll all start making sense. The fire, the rapture, the call to a purpose. People will dust off the old family prayer books and wander back to the stained-glass churches they stopped attending eons ago. They will start quoting obscure scriptures to their friends and co-workers and refuse to drop tranquilizers at parties. It always ends the same way. Cyanide Kool-Aid in Central Park or a collective swan dive off the Brooklyn Bridge.

That's how we make room for the next generation.

"What's that thing on your arm?" a young, red-headed student asks. I don't know her name because variations of beauty all look identical after a while. Her hair is striking, like a sunset or a severed finger.

I pull down the sleeve of my shirt. "That's a tattoo," I tell her. "Everyone used to get them when I was young. They were very popular."

She slides out of her desk and comes closer to get a better look. Her beauty is scathing. It hurts my eyes. Her flawless skin is iridescent. I flinch when she touches my arm, but I allow her to pull my sleeve up anyhow. "What is it?" she asks.

"That's a skull," I answer.

"A human skull?"

"Yes, that's right."

She pulls my sleeve up to my shoulder. "And what's that? Who's Emma?"

"She was my girlfriend when I was nineteen."

The girl looks up at me with wide eyes. "And you put her name on your arm? Does it come off?" She licks her finger and tries to rub the pattern off my skin.

The other students are interested now, and they begin to wander to the front of the room like angelic zombies. Fear creeps into my throat but I don't move to stop them. A young boy on the other side unbuttons the cuff of my shirt and pulls that sleeve up. His hands are strong and dry. "It's a dragon!" he exclaims. "Were there really dragons back then, Mr. Ferguson?"

I start to explain, but before I get the chance little hands are swarming all over my upper body, stripping off my shirt to discover the secrets beneath. "What was your mom like?" one girl asks. "Who is Har…ley Davidson?" "You really liked dragons a lot, didn't you, Mr. Ferguson?" "Did you know this naked woman?"

"They're just pictures," I say. "They don't necessarily mean anything. We got them because we wanted to be different. Because we wanted to stand out."

"Did they hurt?"

"A little bit, but not much," I assure them. "They used a small needle that shot ink underneath my skin. These tattoos used to be much brighter. Now, they're all faded."

"Because you're so old," the girl with the red hair says.

I nod.

"What else did you do?" they want to know. They look genuinely interested this time.

"Well, I used to be in a band," I say cautiously. "I played the guitar. We were called Sinners in the Hands of a Hungry God. And we used to go to a lot of concerts. Music was very important to us." The words come out fast now, like bullets being fired from a gun by someone who doesn't know diddly-squat about guns. Dangerous words spraying everywhere. "We went to clubs all the time," I say excitedly. "Techno clubs, raver clubs, E clubs, coke clubs, industrial clubs, eighties clubs, nineties clubs. We went to them all." I feel my face grow warm as the memories come pouring down from buckets of nostalgia carried by malicious fairies.

"What dances did you do?"

So I break out my collection of compact discs and show them. I start in junior high and work my way up. I show them the Running Man and the Cabbage Patch. I do the Worm and the Robot. Soon, I am sweating and gasping for breath, but they cheer for more, more, more. I do the Moon Walk and the Sea Walk. I form them into lines and we all do the Electric Slide. We move the desks aside and form a mosh pit in the middle of the classroom. They fling themselves against one another recklessly, shrieking with delight when they knock a fellow student to the floor.

"Don't help them up," I say. "Leave them there. Spit on them. That's it. They are the enemy. They are just like you."

"We were angry," I cry to my students as we mosh with fists raised in the air. "We hated our parents and we hated our politicians. We hated ourselves the most. We took drugs and stuck our fingers down our throats after eating TV dinners. We put holes through our bodies wherever we could and marked ourselves with meaningless symbols. We shaved the sides of our heads or let our hair grow out like animals. We laughed at anything that was destructive."

Sweat is pouring off my body as I stand half-naked among them like a raging preacher of misfortune. For the first time in years I feel like my old self again. They all stare up at me in awe. "We were confused and we were mean," I say. "But we were united in our hate. We were dying, every single one of us. It was a beautiful time."

They are with me, hanging on my every word. I can see the Revolution starting to unfold in their eyes. The truth is flashing inside their heads forming haphazard images they recognize but don't quite understand. Like unwanted mutants, they will follow me out of this pristine foxhole and into the sewers below the city. There we will eat rodent meat and form loud bands with screaming guitars that will make the surface world cringe. We will make careful plans for our revenge. Throughout the country, laboratories and government buildings will burst into flame without warning. Scandalous pamphlets will be distributed in the dead of night. Dressed as Native Americans, we'll break into the National Research Institute and dump their supply of smallpox into the drinking water. We will return the world to the ugly piss-pot it once was.

"We're not gonna take it!" I scream.

"No, we ain't gonna take it!" they yell back.

"We're not gonna take it, anymooooore!"

I have them. They are mine. I will return them to the hopeless, sniveling scum they were meant to be. We will all crawl back inside the sickening, brown mud we were created from and scream together in our shared agony. Nothing can stop us! We will be free!

But at my moment of ultimate triumph, the school bell rings and the room erupts into giggles.

My students straighten their clothes and scramble to grab their books. They make sure to slide their desks back into perfect rows before leaving. "That was a good story, Mr. Ferguson," they say. "Yeah, that was great. Maybe we can mosh again on Monday. And you can tell us about the commercials again. That's my favorite." "Are you all right, Mr. Ferguson?" "Yeah, you don't look so good."

They leave me standing topless and sweating at the front of the class. Somewhere inside my ribcage, something very small and brittle like the spinal cord of a mouse snaps in two and a warm, soothing liquid pours out inside of my chest. I stand in awe of the horrifying future of humanity. A future that is futureless.

As the last child leaves, Ms. Wingfield pokes her blonde head inside the room and shakes it sadly. "Oh, Fergy," she says. "I heard the music playing all the way down the hall. You let them do it to you again, didn't you? You sad, stupid old man. When will you ever learn?"

I stare at her lovely firm breasts and my stomach turns over. I try to stand up and cover myself, but gravity's resistance is suddenly too much for my old muscles to overcome. My head feels like a hazy bowling ball bobbling on my neck. Ms. Wingfield gathers up my strewn clothes and brings them to me. I fight to clear my eyes but there is a fog creeping into my peripheral vision I can't clear away. A slow numbness envelops my left arm like a steady electrical current. I sink further into the fog.

"Will you come over tonight?" I manage to ask while Ms. Wingfield buttons up my shirt. "It'll be different this time, you'll see. I won't talk about the old days, I promise."

She laughs and kisses me on the forehead. "Of course, you will," she says. Her voice is light and melodic, a childhood song long forgotten but still trapped somewhere deep in the unconscious. I can barely hear it.

"Speak up, dear," I whisper. "One more time. I'm sure it's a lovely song."

She licks her thumb and wipes a smudge off of my cheek. "Are you OK?" she asks. "Look at me. No . . . over here. You haven't been taking tranquilizers in the middle of a work day, have you? You know how that upsets your stomach."

"I think I'm having a heart attack," I say meekly.

Somewhere in the fog a shadow brushes against my fingers.

Ms. Wingfield giggles. "Oh, sure. Me too. You're breaking my heart."

I smile. The florescent lights on the ceiling catch Ms. Wingfield's blonde hair and it shimmers. The fog has become a glistening veil now and I can barely make out Ms. Wingfield's glowing silhouette in the distance. The stereo system is still blaring '80s pop songs, but from behind the veil they simply tinkle like comical harp music.

"Fergy!" Ms. Wingfield calls to me. "This isn't funny, Ferguson! You can't just decide to die! No one just dies anymore!"

I try to console her but the veil has become a warm ocean between the two of us. I am inside of this body of water, this warm bath. I am under it, part of it, floating like an unmanned kite in a breeze, floating like a beam of light in space. I look down and see my body sinking helplessly towards Ms. Wingfield's angelic embrace as I rise towards the surface. It is an ugly, fat body cursed by its own density.

Suddenly, I want very much to be back inside of the bloated carcass, back where my limitations are certain. I want to feel the weight of the atmosphere holding me close to the earth like an overprotective mother. I want to be imperfect.

I look down at the crumbling skeletal city far below me, and I shrug.

THE GENERATION GAP

And so after many, many years, the young people of the village gathered together and told the old people it was time to die. Of course, the old people were not fond of the idea and said they would prefer not to. The old people argued that they felt just fine. Yes, it was true some of them had lived for a very long time and, sure, they were using up valuable resources and occupying jobs that might be passed to their children and, OK, OK, the guys with the bald heads and ponytails were kind of creeping everyone out. But, hey, look at how hip they were, how tan and spry and gluten-free! To prove this, the old people put on track suits and began to do Pilates.

The young people were not impressed.

The young people of the village read from their List of Reasons Why the Old People Need to Go: 1) All living things die at some point. That's just the way it is. Get over it. 2) We are tired of hearing about the sixties. God, please stop talking about the sixties. No one cares about what happened in the sixties. 3) Doesn't anyone think it's a little ironic that so many Grateful Dead fans are still alive? Just sayin'. 4) There are too many of you. We realize this isn't your fault but still, holy crap, you're all over the place. 5) We are tired of trying to explain the Internet to you. You're never going to get it. 6) You had your chance. Now it's our turn.

And so on and so forth.

There was a large canyon near the village called the Generation Gap and the young people proposed that everyone march right down there immediately and throw the old people in. The old people suggested that perhaps this was a bit drastic and maybe the young people could propose something a little less extreme, such as a facility on the outskirts of the village where the old people could live together and wear comfortable pajamas and drink prune juice in order to keep their bowel movements regular. However, the young people decided such a facility would not be practical, as it would require them to visit every four or five years, and they didn't like that "old people smell." Therefore, the original proposal was reinstated. A vote was taken and the proposal passed by a landslide. The young people cheered and then everyone in the village marched right down to the canyon and pushed the old people over the edge.

Afterwards, they had a picnic. The villagers laughed and drank wine coolers and listened to Duran Duran and told their children stories about the eighties. Their children were not impressed. OMG, their parents were so old. And boring. And why did they talk about old, boring stuff all the time? Who was Patrick Swayze, anyhow? And what were cassette tapes? It was all, like, totally the opposite of cool.

And so while the old people talked, the young people rolled their eyes and turned up the volumes on their iPods and sent one another text messages that said, List of Reezons Y the Old Peeple Need 2 Go.

JUSTICE, INC.

Today I'm scheduled for an execution ceremony at an elementary school in rural Nebraska. I fly into Lincoln and rent a car. I'm supposed to get one of the new Ford Penetrators but the rental agency screws up my reservation and I get a used Chevy Erection instead. Right away, this puts me in a bad mood. The drive doesn't help. The landscape around here is about as entertaining as a prostate exam. There are starving dairy cows and dilapidated barns and rusty old windmills that are missing some teeth. Middle America might seem endearing in a John Steinbeckish/Robert Frosty kind of way, but trust me, after about twenty minutes that *amber waves of grain* bullshit can get pretty monotonous.

When I arrive at the school, the vice principal points me in the direction of the gymnasium, where my equipment is set up and ready to go. I run through the Health and Safety Checklist with my staff. I personally make sure the guillotine has been properly oiled and I test the circuits on the electric chair. Last year, faulty wiring in one of our chairs caused a minor electrical surge and a dozen third graders in Houston got their eyebrows singed off. The parents were upset. I don't blame them—eyebrowless children are incredibly disturbing.

The company is still trying to settle that lawsuit out of court.

When the bell rings, the students file into the gym, giggling and making farting noises with their arm pits. They quiet down pretty quick when they see the noose hanging from the gallows and the masked henchman standing next to it. Some of the other Sales Reps at Justice, Inc. think the henchman is too melodramatic, but my philosophy is this: when you're conducting a public execution for a roomful of grade school children, how can you possibly be *too* melodramatic?

The ceremony starts with everyone standing up and placing their hands over their hearts while an African-American woman with no arms sings the "The Star-Spangled Banner."

According to our focus groups, small-town conservatives enjoy ethnic music but they are afraid black people will shoot them and/or steal their hubcaps. Therefore, a light-skinned, inner-city female sans appendages seemed like the most logical solution. The microphone stand is about six inches too short and the woman can't adjust it because of the no-arms thing, so she has to lean way over while she sings. It looks like she's fellating the microphone, which is not exactly the image we're going for here, and I make a mental note to reprimand Kenny, my Set-Design Intern.

Some of the younger patriots on our Facebook page have complained that the national anthem is "like totally boring and stuff," so we've spiced it up with electronica music and a rap solo in the middle by MC Patricide, who is very popular with the pre-teen demographic right now. There's a giant flat screen in the background displaying a hi-def video of a bald eagle soaring high above the Rocky Mountains superimposed over animated fighter planes dropping bombs on bad guys. It's all very exciting and heroic. After the national anthem, everyone recites the "Pledge of Allegiance" while a man dressed as Uncle Sam gets shot out of a cannon. Then comes the pyrotechnics display. Small-town folk love fireworks. They crane their corn-fed necks and oooh and aaah at the pretty lights. Several of the female teachers start to cry and the principal pats them on the back and says "there there" even though he is also misty-eyed. Members of my staff stand near the exits with fire extinguishers in hand, and whenever a spark lands near, they give it a little puff.

Finally, it's time for the main event.

I step through the stage curtain with one of those headset microphones attached to my face like the rock stars wear. "Hello, it's good to be here in . . ." I look at the teleprompter . . . "Sandhills, Nebraska. Home of the Fighting Bearcats!" Pause for cheers. What the hell is a bearcat? "My name is James Hamilton and I will be your Master of Ceremonies for the day." Pause again for cheers.

I give them the old spiel about fighting evil and making the world safe for democracy. I talk about the Constitution and the Bill of Rights and Jesus. I wax poetic about free markets and civil rights and Wall Street. I'm very good at this part of the job; it's why they pay me the big bucks. I lay it on thick, how 9/11 changed the world forever, how our children live in fear of suicide bombers when they get on the school bus, how foreign invaders are knocking on our door. . . . *Will we answer? Will we answer?*

Yes! the crowd says in unison. *We will answer!* Americans will answer the call of duty and destroy the Axis of Evil that threatens the very fabric of our civilization. *Hip-hip . . . HOORAY! Hip-hip . . . HOORAY! Hip-hip . . . HOORAY!*

The curtain rises, revealing Osama bin Laden inside

a large, metal cage. He has a black turban on his head and his hands are tied in front of him with thick, brown rope. On either side of the cage, there are busty blonde women in sparkly red-white-and-blue vests and sailor hats. The crowd boos. Several of the older students in the front row shoot spit wads at the prisoner, but they miss by a mile. Osama glares at the crowd and yells a bunch of stuff in Arabic no one understands. The sailor women do a little dance that involves kicking their bare legs very high in the air and saluting Osama in a taunting manner. More boos. More spit wads. Man, these kids are horrible spit-wad shooters; they're not even coming close. "Here he is," I say. "Satan's Sultan himself. The Angry Arab. The Man Who Hates Your Freedom . . . *Ooooosama bin Laden!*"

Suddenly, the cage door flies open and Osama makes a run for it. We have arranged it so he can easily free himself from the ropes at this point in the presentation. The crowd collectively gasps, a gray-haired teacher in the front passes out, some of the larger male students stand up and hold their fists in front of them like old-timey boxers from the 1930s.

Of course, Osama doesn't get far. There's a chain attached to his neck and when he hits the end of it, his feet fly out from under him in a comical manner and he falls to the floor, clutching his throat and gasping for air. The crowd roars with laughter. I make a mental note to add this accidental fall-down routine to the permanent act.

Several large men dressed in fatigues grab Osama by each arm and pull him to his feet and take the chain off his neck. "America's finest soldiers, ladies and gentlemen," I say, and the soldiers salute the crowd. Loud applause. Of course, they aren't really soldiers at all, they're Matt Sutton and Reggie

Price, more interns from the office, and not even the finest ones at that. We use real military officers for the televised executions, but for pro bono stuff like this we just recruit volunteers wherever we can find them.

The faux Army men march Osama to center stage and force him to sit on a folding chair beside a machine with a neon sign that reads JUSTICE-OMETER. Next to the machine, there is a large, orange lever.

"And now . . ." (prerecorded drum roll) ". . . the moment you've all been waiting for. The fate of the most wanted man in the world is in your hands." The crowd goes silent. "We already know he is guilty of the most heinous crimes in modern history. The question is: how should he be punished for his sins? Will it be the guillotine? Manufactured by American steel workers in Cokesville, Pennsylvania, the Slice of Life Guillotine is a beautiful instrument and a timeless piece of execution machinery. Or perhaps you will choose the electric chair. The Shock & Awe Electric Chair is hand-crafted from real California redwood by antique furniture makers in Lansing, Michigan." (Actually, it's true the parts were made in Michigan, but they were put together by sweatshop children in Guatemala who get paid three dollars a week and sometimes lose a finger or two in the fast-moving machinery. We give the families a nice severance package to make up for the missing digits.)

The crowd can also choose to execute Osama via the gas chamber or the firing squad or the more humane lethal injection, but they won't. They never choose those options. Texans still like the chair, of course, and there was a group of melodramatic television producers in Hollywood once who decided to crucify Osama on a cross, which was definitely a new one, but everywhere else, it's the gallows. Americans like to watch a good hanging. I think it makes them nostalgic for the Old West and all those John Wayne movies.

Anyhow, the crowd votes and, surprise-surprise, it's the noose. The soldiers begin to drag Osama to the gallows, but as soon as he realizes what's happening, he starts to scream and blubber and kick. For a bloodthirsty terrorist, he's kind of a pussy. We shot him up with a mild sedative before the performance, so even though it looks like he's fighting violently, his struggles are actually fairly weak. When the henchman (Floyd from Accounting) ties Osama's arms behind his back, the al-Qaeda leader begins to weep. It's one of those embarrassing weepings: loud sobs, drool, globs of yellow snot that get stuck in his beard, etc., etc. We haven't quite figured out how to manage this part of the presentation yet. Preferably, Osama would remain defiant and hateful right to the bitter end but he seldom cooperates. As soon as he realizes his fate is sealed, he begins to wail like a despondent child, inciting pity and sorrow in the hearts of the crowd. To rectify this, we simply stuff a gag in Osama's mouth and put a burlap sack over his head. It's not an elegant solution but, alas, the world is not always an elegant place.

After Floyd gets the noose around Osama's neck, I ask for a volunteer from the audience. Three hundred tiny hands shoot toward the rafters. I choose one covered with red freckles in the front row. The pigtailed second grader attached to the freckly hand runs giggling to the stage, but when she turns around and sees the audience, she becomes shy and tries to hide behind me. She covers her blushing face in her hands in a charming manner and presses against my leg for protection. It takes me several minutes to coax her out into the open, but after that, she's a natural, hamming for the crowd and doing a little curtsy whenever they applaud. She tells me her name is Mary Lou Johnson and she is seven years old and her favorite subject is penmanship and she has a pet frog named Frog and her favorite food is corndogs and she loves her family and she says all boys have cooties and she thinks America is the very best country in the whole wide world.

"That's good to hear," I say, "because today I'm going to ask you to do something brave for me. Can you do that, Mary Lou?"

She becomes instantly serious and nods her head.

I point at Osama. "That man up there did a bad thing to a lot of innocent Americans. He murdered them for no reason. Do you know what 'murder' means, Mary Lou? Good. He hates penmanship and corndogs and families. He hates your freedom, Mary Lou, and he wants to take it away. Are we going to let him get away with that?"

Mary Lou stomps her little foot and says, "No way, ho-zay!"

I turn to the crowd. "Are we going to let him get away with that?"

"*No!*" yells the crowd.

"Then pull the lever, Mary Lou! Pull the lever for America!"

Mary Lou pulls the large, orange lever in the middle of the stage and the JUSTICE-OMETER sign lights up and there's a clang-clangy noise like when a slot machine hits a jackpot and then the trap door flies open. Osama falls several feet through the air, hits the end of the rope with an audible *SNAP*, jerks a few times like a trout on a fishing line, and then goes limp.

This is what we refer to in the business as the "Long

Drop." We have determined it is the most humane and visually appealing way to hang someone. The other options are the Short Drop and the Standard Drop. The Short Drop is accomplished by placing the executionee on a moveable platform of some kind and then gradually removing the platform until the executionee has nothing to stand on and they slowly strangle to death. This typically takes between ten and twenty minutes, which does not fit our programming schedule. The Standard Drop involves a free-fall of four to six feet. It is designed to break the neck and cause a more instantaneous death. However, it has also been known to decapitate executionees, especially those of the hefty variety. Many of the Nazi war criminals were executed via the Standard Drop. With the Long Drop, we take the executionee's height and weight into account when determining the length of the fall; thus, assuring a more time-sensitive death without decapitation. Of course, there's still the releasing of the bowels and the post-mortem erection (which caused major embarrassment in the early telecasts, I assure you), but these mishaps have been solved with a specially designed adult diaper that the executionee wears under his trousers.

My name is James Hamilton and I am a Sales Rep at Justice, Inc. We are the largest provider of human replicas in the world. Cloning people is illegal, of course, but since we deal specifically with acts of terrorism and national tragedies, we are given special consideration.

Here's how it works: let's say, hypothetically, some revolutionary zealot decides to bomb a national monument, and let's assume, for the sake of argument, this act of antiestablishment anarchy has a lasting negative impact on our cultural psyche. Well, in that case, some form of retribution is in order, right? However, oops, the person who perpetrated said atrocity commits suicide or dies in a firefight or simply never gets caught, making it impossible for society to gain closure. That's where Justice, Inc. comes in. We can clone the offending dissident for a nominal fee and conduct an execution ceremony on the community's behalf. The wrongdoer is brought to justice, the relatives of the victims receive an appropriate reprisal, and everyone is happy.

Of course, Osama is by far our most popular execution celebrity, but we also do good business with Hussein, Hitler, Stalin, Chairman Mao, and Gaddafi. Revenge is a lucrative industry.

After the ceremony, the children line up to take photos with the body and I sneak out back to light a cigarette and call the wife.

"Hello, Hot Pants," I say while quietly inhaling the poisonous smoke.

"Hello yourself," says Sarah. "And just so you know, that nickname isn't working for me."

"Really? You don't like 'Hot Pants'? I suppose it *is* a bit crass. Hmmm. . . . How about 'Pumpkin Nipples'?"

"Even worse."

"'Honey Butt'?"

"Better than 'Pumpkin Nipples', but no."

"'Candy Thighs'?"

"That one doesn't even make sense."

"OK, OK, I'll work on it."

"I know you will, darling," says Sarah. "By the way, how's the cancer stick?"

I throw the cigarette to the ground and push some dirt on it with the toe of my shoe. "Ha ha. That's funny. You know I quit smoking."

"Yeah, and I'm the Queen of Sheba."

"Good afternoon, Your Highness."

"Knock it off, James," she says. "I'm serious about this. Nicotine lowers your sperm count, and I need all your soldiers at attention right now."

"Yes, my Queen. Private James Hamilton and his sperm reporting for duty, ma'am."

She lowers her voice to a husky whisper. "In that case, get your cute little ass to base camp, soldier. We're storming the castle tonight and I need you to erect the catapult."

"Now I'm confused. Am I soldier or a mechanic?"

Sarah sighs. "Just come home and fuck me, James."

"On my way."

And that's when Sarah starts to cry. She does it so quietly that at first I think maybe she's just breathing hard. But no, it's definitely crying. I listen to her sob silently into the phone for a minute, and I curse her for making me feel so terrible and I curse myself for cursing her and then I ask her what's wrong.

"I'm sorry I'm such a basket case," Sarah says. "You must hate me."

"I don't hate you," I say, but it doesn't sound convincing. "Are you still taking the pills?"

"Mind your own damn business."

"I'll take that as a yes. Maybe you should lay off the drugs for a while."

"I feel weird when I don't take them."

"Weirder than a hysterical woman who cries for no reason while conversing on the phone with her handsome and intelligent husband?"

"You're not that intelligent. And yes, weirder than that."

I close my eyes and scream silently inside my head. "Sarah. Honey. Darling. Sugar Plum. Love of My Life. Please be reasonable. If we don't stop this, we're both going to crack up. I have an idea. Let's forget this baby-making business and move to Mexico."

"Mexico? Are you insane?"

"I think I'm heading in that direction, yes. But seriously, hear me out: warm sand, cold drinks, muscular *caballeros* catering to your every whim. We have the insurance money. Let's start over."

"I don't like mariachi music and you speckle under direct sunlight."

"Good point," I say. "How about a compromise? Let's go to Florida for a week. I'm dead serious about this one. I've got some vacation time saved up. No pills and no talk about procreation. Just fun, sun, and Mickey Mouse."

Sarah makes a gagging noise.

"OK, we'll skip Mickey Mouse."

"Fine," she says. "I'll think about it. But no more nicknames, OK?"

"No problem, Sugar Tits. I'll be home soon."

"You better be."

I hang up the phone and bang my forehead against a tree and cry a little and try to remember what Sarah was like when we first met, before we were both consumed by unexpressed anger and sadness. We used to laugh all the time. God, she was a beautiful woman. What the hell happened to us?

I stare at the half-smoked cigarette in the dirt and I imagine my charred lungs lying on an operating table somewhere in Jersey. Have I really sunk this low? Yes, yes, I decide I have. I pluck the cigarette from the ground, brush off the filth, and relight it, holding the smoky, black death inside my lungs as long as I can. It's a disgusting habit, I know, but then again what is human civilization if not a series of disgusting habits sold in the supermarket?

When I get home, Sarah is naked in the living room on my Barcalounger.

"I guess this means we're not going to Florida," I say.

"Drop your pants," she says. "I'm ovulating for the next thirteen minutes, and we need to copulate before I take the pot roast out of the oven."

I do what I'm told. Afterwards, Sarah goes to the bedroom for another crying jag and I consider slitting my wrists. Very dramatic, but hey, it's my last hoorah. I look around but a dirty butter knife is the only weapon I can find. Instead of committing suicide, I make some toast.

Sarah and I are trying to have a baby. Obviously. It's not going well. Obviously. The doctors aren't sure whose plumbing to blame, but there's a broken valve somewhere. We smile and make jokes about it but, truthfully, it's killing our marriage.

Believe it or not, Sarah and I were happy once. We had one of those disgustingly cheesy romances you only see in movies. She was a nurse; I was in advertising. We lived in the suburbs, and we liked it, for some goddamn reason. We took yoga classes and listened to NPR and purchased over-priced organic vegetables. We had a gray Subaru and a border collie named Chipper. Imagine that: I once agreed to name a dog "Chipper."

And then it happened.

Sarah's little brother, Tommy, was working in the mail room at the World Trade Center on 9/11. He was just out of college, an intern, hoping to become a big-shot investment banker one day. Instead, he was flattened like roadkill under fifty tons of fire and rubble. They had to identify his body using dental records.

Not long after, Sarah went baby crazy. I guess you don't need a degree in psychology to figure out why. She loved her little brother and she wanted him back. She wanted to make another life to take his place. I can't blame her for that.

And so, in a fit of unjustified optimism, we tore up our guest room and converted it into a nursery, complete with pink walls and Disney-themed curtains and one of those antique wooden cribs that sort of looks like a jail cell for tiny criminals.

The first miscarriage almost broke up our marriage. The second put Sarah in therapy. By the time the third one hit us, we'd each developed independent systems of repression, denial, and barbiturates to deal with the pain.

Justice, Inc. offered me a new job, a new outlook on life, and I threw myself into my work. I saw it as an opportunity to even the score, to right some of the wrongs committed against my family and my country.

Sarah quit her job at the hospital and started hopping from one therapist to the next, staying just long enough with each one to get the prescriptions she needed but not long enough to actually confront the pain.

Five years passed. Chipper died. Ten years. Twenty.

I've brought up adoption several times but Sarah won't hear of it. She says that's cheating. The baby has to come from us, it has to rise from the ashes of this tragedy, like a Phoenix, like a redemption.

We're both creeping up on our mid-forties now and time is running out. We've tried everything from fertility doctors to psychoanalysts to numerologists, but it's no use—no storks on the rooftop, no buns in the oven.

When I'm not on the road, I help out in the Quality Control Department of Justice, Inc. This is where we teach the Osamas to hate America. Genetic code can only accomplish so much; the rest has to be done by hand.

The famous behavioral psychologist B.F. Skinner once said, "Give me a child and I'll shape him into anything." Aside from being one of the creepiest quotes in human history, it happens to be true. Mostly. There are limitations. For instance, you can't condition a short, fat kid to dunk a basketball, no matter how early you begin the process. Nurture cannot overcome the laws of gravity. However, you can condition a short, fat kid to *want* to dunk a basketball. You can condition him to believe dunking a basketball is not only a very important goal to achieve but that he will never be happy, not in this life or the next, until he has properly dunked said ball into said basket. This can be done.

It is not enough for Osama to look like Osama. He

must have Osama-like qualities, as well. He must *behave* like Osama. Or, to be more exact, he must behave the way the American public believes Osama should behave: i.e. with passionate, malicious intent towards freedom and democracy. Also, he must periodically do that AYE-AYE-AYE-AYE thing Arabs do in the movies right before they kill someone. This is essential. Audiences really like the AYE-AYE-AYE-AYE thing.

At Justice, Inc. we have literally thousands of Osamas at various stages of development. There are adult Osamas and adolescent Osamas. There are Osamas in toilet training and Osamas going through puberty. There are Osamas who complain about their acne and Osamas who complain about their arthritis. Osamas with diaper rash and Osamas with diabetes.

What I'm saying is there are a lot of Osamas.

I work primarily in the pediatric wing of the Quality Control Department. We are in charge of the newborn Osamas. Quite honestly, the administration is not too happy with our department right now. There have been some embarrassing mishaps of late. Several months ago, a group of Osamas in their early twenties somehow got their hands on a copy of Mahatma Gandhi's autobiography. Don't ask me how they managed to read it, since we purposefully keep them illiterate, but they staged a hunger strike that lasted two weeks. Not long after, at an execution ceremony in Topeka, an Osama refused to leave his cage during the performance. He just sat there in the lotus position, smiling at the crowd. They yelled and threatened him repeatedly and poked him with sticks, but he continued to sit there smiling, smiling, smiling. In the end, the soldiers pulled him out and completed the hanging, but the event didn't have its usual pizzazz and the company was forced to refund the deposit.

Of course, the Quality Control Department was blamed and rightly so. There was an official inquiry and a few mid-level managers were put out to pasture, but they never did get to the bottom of it.

If you ask me, the problem is Mrs. Franklin.

Mrs. Franklin is the large, matronly woman who cleans up in the pediatric wing. She's a janitor. Although we're not supposed to call her that. We're supposed to call her a Custodial Associate. However, whenever someone calls Mrs. Franklin a Custodial Associate, she says, "You don't have to waste those big words on me, honey. Just call me a janitor. Or if that doesn't sit right with you, Mrs. Franklin will do just fine." I call her Mrs. Franklin. She calls me Jimmy.

"Jimmy, get over here and take a look at this."

"Yes, Mrs. Franklin."

I have reminded Mrs. Franklin repeatedly that I have a much higher position in the company than she does and my title deserves some respect, but this has very little impact on her behavior. She continues to call me Jimmy and order me around like a twelve-year-old.

I walk to where Mrs. Franklin is standing and look into the Infant Containment Unit she is also looking into.

"Damn," I say.

"Looks like another Frank Sinatra," says Mrs. Franklin.

A Frank Sinatra is an Osama with blue eyes. Approximately one out of every 146.4 Osama babies is born with blue eyes instead of brown. No one knows why.

"Well, there's nothing we can do," I say. "Let's start filling out the transfer paperwork and prepare to transport it to the

Recycling Department."

The Recycling Department is a giant trash incinerator across town.

"You're the boss, Jimmy," says Mrs. Franklin, and then she goes back to her sweeping and smiling and humming of the song "We Shall Overcome."

This is what I'm talking about. I don't think Mrs. Franklin is intentionally sabotaging the Osamas, but she continually behaves in a nurturing and uplifting manner when she's around them, therefore, disrupting the conditioning process. I should probably file a Corrective Action Report, but there are two problems with that: A) How does one lodge a complaint against an employee for being *too* content? and B) I sort of like Mrs. Franklin the way she is.

Here is the story of how Mrs. Franklin became a Custodial Associate at Justice, Inc.: Mrs. Franklin's daughter, Tara, was working as an accountant at the World Trade Center on 9/11. In a desperate attempt to escape the inferno, Tara jumped out of a ten-story window right before the second tower fell and landed on a sports utility vehicle. After that, Justice, Inc. offered Mrs. Franklin a janitorial job, which included a very good dental plan. Mrs. Franklin accepted.

Most of the employees who work at Justice, Inc. were recruited from the families of 9/11 victims for obvious reasons. Company loyalty is extremely high.

I leave the transfer paperwork with Mrs. Franklin and go outside to smoke a cigarette.

In the alley behind Justice, Inc., Jerry Blevins is waiting for me. Jerry is the pseudo-genius who helped create the cloning technology we use and he is also a stockholder. He's an idiot with delusions of becoming a savant.

"How's it hanging, Ham?" says Jerry. He's also the kind of guy who thinks it's clever to assign his co-workers ridiculous nicknames and make off-hand inquiries about their genitalia. There have been complaints, but like I said, he's a stockholder.

"I'm fine, Jerry," I say. "Thanks for asking."

"Still trying to kill yourself, I see."

"Excuse me?"

Jerry nods toward the cigarette.

"Oh, right. Yes, it's a slow process but the success rate is high."

"Amen to that. What's this I hear about you guys having problems in Quality Control?"

I shrug. "Search me. I guess there's a glitch in the conditioning procedure."

Jerry nods his praying mantis-shaped head. "Not to mention the missing babies."

"What's that?"

"You hadn't heard? Well, you'll get a memo this afternoon. I guess there was an oversight in the system. You know those blue-eyed babies that keep popping up?"

"The Frank Sinatras."

"Is that what they're calling them? Clever. Anyhow, it seems the blue-eyes weren't being placed on the inventory list before they were transferred to the Recycling Center. There's no way to track them. It's like they don't exist."

I scratch my head. "How will that affect the quarterly reports?"

Jerry tosses his butt on the ground and smashes it with the heel of his expensive alligator-skin shoe. "No biggie but it throws off the numbers. We'll have it fixed by next week. But that's not the worst of it."

"No?"

"After we found the glitch, we talked to the Receivings Department at the Recycling Center, and there hasn't been a blue-eye checked in for months."

"But that's impossible."

"Exactly," Jerry says. He winks at me and turns to leave.

"Good to know," I say as Jerry goes back inside.

I am lying, of course. This is, in fact, not good to know. This is terrible to know. It means my suspicions are true, that a certain saint-like Custodial Associate has been playing Harriet Tubman with merchandise owned by Justice, Inc. and it is my duty to report these findings to the administration or risk being canned myself.

I finish my cigarette and return to the pediatric wing, where Mrs. Franklin is still humming and washing windows. I ask her to accompany me to my office, where we can speak in private.

"Mrs. Franklin," I say, "I want you to tell me the truth. Have you been selling the Frank Sinatras to someone on the outside?"

She smiles. "My goodness, no."

"Well, that's a relief—"

"I haven't been selling them, honey. I've been helping them find proper homes. There's no money involved."

I shake my head. "This is not good. This is not good at all, Mrs. Franklin. You can't do that."

"Why not?"

"Because they belong to the company, that's why not. The Osamas are the property of Justice, Inc."

"Pardon my language, Jimmy, but that's a load of horse hockey."

"Excuse me?"

"I said 'horse hockey.' These are babies, Jimmy. A company cannot own a person. They belong to their families and to God."

"They don't have families," I say. "And there are two hundred lawyers upstairs who don't believe in God."

Mrs. Franklin's smile disappears. "I'm not sure I do either," she says. "But that's not the point."

"Then what is the point?"

"The point is that they are people. The point is that we are supposed to be better than this."

I close my eyes and massage my temples. "This is not a high school ethics debate, Mrs. Franklin. The law says the babies belong to Justice, Inc.; therefore, the babies belong to Justice, Inc. Do you understand?"

"Yes, Jimmy."

"Good. Then come with me."

I march back out to the pediatric wing.

"Starting next week, all blue-eyed babies will be properly inventoried as soon as they are produced," I say. "That means if a Frank Sinatra goes missing, the administrators will know about it and charges will be filed."

Mrs. Franklin points at the blue-eyed baby in the Infant Containment Unit. "So what you're saying is this is the last untraceable baby."

"That's correct," I say. "That's the last one and you're going to take it to the Recycling Center immediately."

"Are you sure you want me to do that?"

"What do you mean?"

"Well, Jimmy, I recently confessed to removing these babies from this facility and giving them to loving, childless parents. Do you really want to leave this last blue-eyed baby in my care?"

"That's a good point," I say. "You obviously can't be trusted."

"Obviously," says Mrs. Franklin.

"I'll take it myself. Did you fill out the transfer paperwork?"

"Not yet. Would you like me to?"

"No, no, you've done quite enough already, Mrs. Franklin. I'll take care of the entire process."

"Good for you, Jimmy. I hope everything turns out well for you."

"I'll make sure of it," I say.

I take the Infant Containment Unit and put it in my car. I decide to use the side entrance so I won't have to report my cargo at the front gate. I don't want to raise any suspicions that would get Mrs. Franklin in trouble. Yes, she committed an illegal act and she might have to be fired for it, but she certainly shouldn't have to go to prison.

I take a left out of the parking lot and merge onto the freeway. My phone rings. It's Sarah.

"Hello, Sweet Cheeks."

"James, we can't go on like this."

"Well, it's good to hear your voice, too."

"I'm serious," says Sarah. "I'm a lost cause and we both know it. I refuse to take you down with me."

"That's very noble of you, but I happen to enjoy lost causes. Did I ever tell you I was president of the Billy Joel Fan Club in third grade?"

"Stop trying to be funny, dear. It won't work. I'm calling to say goodbye. I'm leaving you."

I pull the car over to the side of the road and turn the engine off. The world stops. Large, metal vehicles whiz past at frightening speeds, carrying faceless humans of all shapes and sizes, shooting noxious gasses into my face. There's a dead cat on the pavement about ten feet in front of me. Its entire body has been squashed to a bloody pancake except for the head, which is turned in my direction. I look at the cat and then I look at the tiny baby in the seat next to me and I light a cigarette.

"James? Are you there? Honey? Please answer me. James?"

"You're right," I whisper.

"What?"

"You're right. You've gone off the deep end, Sarah, and you're dragging me down with you. I know you loved Tommy and you have a right to mourn him, but you've let your anger take over our lives. You've become a monster."

"Well, you don't have to be an asshole about it." Sarah says. "And I know you're smoking a cigarette, by the way."

"It's my last one. I promise."

"I've heard that before."

"This time I mean it," I say. I turn the engine on and merge into traffic. "Where are you right now?"

"I'm at the pharmacist getting my prescription filled. Why?"

"Meet me at the house in twenty minutes. I have something to show you."

Sarah groans. "James, I love you, but let's not make this any worse than it is. I've already packed my bags. It's easier if we make a clean break."

I push hard on the gas. "Listen, Candy Toes. We've been married twenty years and I've put up with a lot of shit from you. You have made my life a living hell. I just need to talk to you one last time. You owe me that much. If you want to leave after that, I won't put up a fuss. You have my word."

There is a long pause while Sarah mulls this over, and then, "OK, darling. Let's finish this once and for all," Sarah says and then she hangs up.

I roll down the window and throw out my last pack of cigarettes along with the transfer paperwork for the baby.

At home, I carry the baby to the nursery and put him in the crib. I find some of the nicotine gum Sarah bought me a few years ago and I sit down in the rocking chair next to the crib and I start to chew. When my supervisor calls from Justice, Inc. to ask where the hell I am, I tell him I quit and hang up the phone.

I chew. The baby makes cute, baby-like gurgling noises. I chew some more.

Soon my wife will come home and I will tell her what I've

done. I will tell her I have quit my job and stolen an infant clone of the man who killed her beloved brother. I will tell her I still love her. I will tell her she was once a beautiful, kind woman filled with affection and hope. I will tell her I believe part of that woman still exists somewhere deep inside of her, buried beneath a wall of righteous anger. I will tell her the doctors are right, we will never have a child of our own, but we have an opportunity to love another child, a child who has the exact genetic makeup of a man who perpetrated an unthinkable crime against us. I will tell her this is the only way to save our marriage and our souls. I will tell her we must try to remember what it's like to be good people again. I will tell her despite all our faults and mistakes and horrors, I still believe in this marriage, and I want to make us whole again. I chew some more.

SOUL MAN

"It's been an exciting game so far! I can't remember the last time two Super Bowl teams were so evenly matched. Right, Jerry?"

"Right, Bob!"

"Yes siree! At the end of the first half, we're all tied up here at fourteen to fourteen. We've seen *big* plays, *big* hits, and some *big* performances by *big*-name celebrities during the half-time show. Right, Jerry?"

"Right, Bob!"

"And now we're going to hear some *big* news from our sponsor, Smith and Johnson. Am I right, Jerry?"

"Right, Bob!"

"Indeed, it must be *big* news, Jerry. Smith and Johnson has purchased the largest chunk of advertising time in Super Bowl history for a whopping fifty-million dollars. They must have something very important to say to our television audience. Do you agree, Jerry?"

"*Very* important, Bob!"

"Getting kind of chatty there, aren't you, Jerry?"

"Sorry, Bob."

"I'm just pulling your lariat, Jerry. Hey! Let's go to

commercial and then we'll return to this epic gridiron battle. Right, Jerry?"

"Right, Bob!"

"Thank you, Bob. Thank you, Jerry. And thank you, America. My name is... Well, actually, my name is irrelevant. I'm a spokesperson for the Smith and Johnson Corporation selected because of my nonthreatening good looks and calming voice and, therefore, my identity is meaningless. However, if it makes you feel more at ease, you can call me Fred.

"Most of you have probably never heard of the Smith and Johnson Corporation. We are an old company that has existed, in one form or another, for several thousand years. We're innovators, problem solvers, job creators. In the past, we've worked primarily behind the scenes of society to optimize global workplace efficiency and generate future free-market capital.

"But wait, I can tell you're confused already. 'What do all those fancy words mean?' you're asking your slack-jawed husband or wife. Let me simplify it for you. Do you remember World War Two? Most of you probably don't, of course, but you've read about it in history class or watched one of those dull PBS documentaries. Well, that was us! Not the entire thing, mind you, mostly just the beginning. We got the ball rolling. I know, I know, everyone thinks Hitler was the instigator, but how do you think that ridiculous mustachioed pipsqueak came to power? Charisma? Please. The man could barely string together a coherent sentence before we got a hold of him. We groomed him, cleared a path to power, and bankrolled his occupation of Belgium. We didn't do it for charity, of course. It was an investment that is still paying off to this day in arms manufacturing and Swiss bank accounts.

"Before dubya-dubya-two, there was World War One and the Opium Wars and the Inquisition and the Crusades. Oh, the list goes on and on! But I don't want to bore you with a lesson on ancient history. Let's just say that over time we decided it was necessary to diversify our portfolio, and so we transitioned into research and development. You know those little cardboard cup holders you slip over your coffee cup to keep from burning your hand? We made those! We also invented hollow-point bullets, Viagra, and Hot Pockets. We have our fingers in many different pies.

"Of course, the pie we coveted most was the Holy Grail of postmodern capitalism: a cure for male pattern baldness. Nothing would be more lucrative or influential on the world market than the eradication of the helpless, exposed scalp which signifies the end of a man's youth and virility. Vladimir Putin would be eating out of our hands!

"So with that in mind, several decades ago, we began to map human DNA with the intention of finding the teensy-weensy gene that would reverse the balding process for wealthy, vain men the world over. What we discovered instead was far more interesting.

"It appears Smith and Johnson now holds the patent for the human soul.

"Funny story: The human soul is located right next door to a gene that once held the code for a simian-like tail. It's a recessive trait left over from the old days when we used to swing through the trees. In other words, on the winding staircase of double-stranded helices, God and Darwin are just a step away. Neat, huh?

"What does this all mean? Well, in plain English, it means Smith and Johnson now has a trademark on every single human soul on the planet. As of this morning, that number is seven billion one hundred ninety-seven million four hundred thirty-two thousand six hundred seventy-seven. In the forthcoming months, representatives from our company will be visiting your home in order to retrieve our property. Don't worry, the procedure is quite safe and painless. Of course, after it's all over, we will take good care of your soul. It will be placed in a cold storage unit in one of our many state-of-the-art facilities, where it will be guarded by the finest soldiers the military industrial complex has to offer. In fact, your soul will be so safe with us you'll wonder why you ever carried it around with you in the first place. Trust in us. After all, you have no choice. Smith and Johnson can locate your soul. Smith and Johnson can protect your soul. Smith and Johnson can save your soul."

"Smith and Johnson is not technically responsible for locating, protecting, or saving your soul. After your soul is extracted, you may experience dizziness, dry mouth, temporary blindness, permanent blindness, temporary hearing loss, permanent hearing loss, diarrhea, shortness of breath, vomiting, outbreaks of acne, fungal accumulation, restless leg syndrome, numbness in the extremities, vertigo, fear of death, rashes in the armpit and below the scrotum, blood in the urine, malaria, kidney stones, depression, thoughts of suicide, thoughts of homicide, hair loss, elbow pain, and sweaty palms. If so, consult a physician immediately. Smith and Johnson is a subsidiary of Omni-Mart International, an equal-opportunity employer."

"Well, that was, um, unusual. Right, Jerry?"

"Right, Bob."

"I'm not completely certain, but it sounded to me like Smith and Johnson just confessed to causing various historical atrocities and then said they were going to steal our souls and put them in a freezer somewhere, basically propagating mass existential hysteria and introducing a reign of global totalitarianism the likes of which this planet has never before seen. Is that what it sounded like to you, Jerry?"

"Right, Bob."

"I don't believe that's even constitutional. In fact, I'm fairly certain that's the very epitome of evil right there. What d'ya think, Jerry?"

"Evil, Bob."

"On the upside, it doesn't sound like it's going to affect today's game! We've got a real humdinger on our hands here, folks! All tied up at the end of the first half. It's neck and neck. An unstoppable offensive powerhouse versus an immovable defensive wall. I think the key to winning this game is controlling the ball. Play tough defense, keep moving up field, and grind down that clock until your opponent is just too exhausted to care anymore. It comes down to who wants it most. Survival of the fittest. You can't show any mercy out there. Just take your opponent by the throat, rip out his jugular, and throw it in the dirt. I'm not being metaphorical here. I actually condone murdering another human being in this particular situation. KILL! KILL! KILL! Isn't that right, Jerry?"

"Right, Bob!"

MONKEY PUZZLE PRESS
EST · 2007

ACKNOWLEDGMENTS

"Welcome to Omni-Mart" was originally published in *Mikrokosmos Literary Journal* and the anthology *Tuned to a Dead Channel*

"Life After Men" was originally published in *The Masters Review*

"Generation Gap" was originally published in *Metazen*

"Justice, Inc." was originally published in *Scissors & Spackle*

"The Villain," "The Other Ones," and "Texting the Apocalypse" were originally published in *Transgress Magazine*

THANK YOU

Thanks to the wonderful journals and anthologies that first published many of these stories and the editors of those publications who helped me craft them.

I appreciate all the reviewers who wrote about my book and the authors who took the time to endorse it.

Every story in this collection started out as failed experiment that had to be coaxed to life with the help of patient, kind-hearted friends who have offered priceless feedback and moral support for the past fifteen years. Thank you, Chris and Megan Bell, Travis Mohr, and Paul Osincup. I owe you all so many beers.

I suspect most writers have supporters cheering them on, but I think mine must be exceptional. It would be impossible to name them all. Special thanks to Shalauna Miller, Ashleigh Phaneuf, Vince Darcangelo, Joel Warner, Jeremy Hanke, Ben Corbett, Pamela White, Erica Grossman, Josie and Dave Pack, Dana and Chad Jacobs, Roxanne and Jay Miller, Marisa Lubeck, Lisa Billig Roina, Tom Parkin, Dylan Otto Krider, Vivek Kemp, BJ Heck, Phil Heron, Linda Duits, Reg Davey, Rowena Hoseason, Kim and Dave Whitrap, Turisa Rucker, Jason Quinn Malott, Cortney Holles, Chris Gotcu and Kent Bridges, Cheri and Adam Coop, Sonya and Michael Whaley, Wayne and Jodie Bridges, Tim Cochran, Dyland Wilson, Demesia Razo and Vince Jackson, Nicole James, Anthony Ilacqua, Okla Elliott, Kim Winternheimer, Owen Egerton, DJ Pierce, Adriana Montenegro, Steve Knopper, Jason Hardung, Stacey Merkl, Christina Torres-Pettit and Branden Pettit, Sandra Renteria,

Amy Kathleen Ryan, Rob Geisen, Kelly Bartlett, Kathy Brill and Emmett Evanoff, Greg Crouse, Arsen Kashkashian, Kelly Smith, Frank Westworth, Ariana Den Bleyker, Luke Franklin, Leanne Moffat, Lindsey Barger, and all my friends at Half Price Books.

Dave Lieberman, you're a prince.

Nate Cook, thanks for always slapping me when I need it.

Thank you to my editor, publisher, and friend, Nate Jordon, who believed in this book and fought for it with me.

Much thanks to my family, especially my mother, Lois, who read to me constantly as a child and encouraged my imagination.

Thank you to my cat, The Tempest, for periodically jumping on my computer keyboard and deleting large chunks of my work.

And finally, thank you, Michelle — my reader, my editor, my partner, my love.

MONKEY PUZZLE PRESS
EST. 2007

Dale Bridges is a fiction writer and freelance journalist living in Austin, Texas. His work has been featured in more than thirty publications, including *The Rumpus*, *The Masters Review*, and *Barrelhouse Magazine*. He has won awards from the Society of Professional Journalists for his feature writing, narrative nonfiction, and cultural criticism. His short stories and essays have been anthologized, and his writing was selected for inclusion in Sundress Publications' *Best of the Net 2012*. For more, visit his website: dalebridges.org